Obadiah Watson is not accustomed to abrupt answers to prayer.

Lord, I know that You need single men in your service, but I grow weary of working alone for You. I ask only for someone to love—someone who will love me in return. Other men find wives; why can't I?

His sad eyes scanned the female faces in the crowd. There were sweet faces, cross faces, attractive faces, homely faces, old or young faces—not one face that captured him, not one face that—

He froze. Not five feet away she stood. Her silvery blue eyes knocked him for a loop—yet it was not their beauty alone that stunned him. He felt as though he knew her, and she also seemed to recognize him.

She smiled slightly before looking away. She was searching for someone in the crowd. Evidently his had not been the face she sought. He swallowed hard and blinked.

She was the loveliest woman he had ever beheld. Clad in a blue plaid traveling suit and a plumed hat, dark hair modestly coiled at the nape of her neck, she held a bandbox in one hand and a reticule in the other. She was not slender, but neither was she plump. In Obie's opinion, her shape and size were perfect. She was not too young; he judged her age at midthirties.

Lord. . . ? but he dared not complete the question even in his thoughts. Could this woman be the immediate answer to his prayer?

JILL STENGL currently lives in North Carolina but her family has plans to move to Wisconsin and hopes to build a log home. She considers herself a homebody and enjoys home schooling the three oldest of her four children, sewing, drawing, and taking long walks with her husband and Fritz, a miniature schnauzer. Jill writes inspirational romance because that's what she most enjoys reading, and she believes that everything she does should be glorifying to God.

Books by Jill Stengl

HEARTSONG PRESENTS
HP197—Eagle Pilot
HP222—Finally, Love
HP292—A Child of Promise

Time
for a Miracle

Jill Stengl

Heartsong Presents

With love to my second set of parents, Dick and Donajean Stengl. Your love and support for me are one of God's special gifts. Thanks for raising such a wonderful son, too!

Thank you to Paula Pruden-Macha, Virginia Macha, and Peggy Arensmeyer for your criticisms and great advice. I couldn't have written this book without you, my dear friends. God is very good.

A note from the author:
I love to hear from my readers! You may correspond with me by writing: **Jill Stengl**
Author Relations
PO Box 719
Uhrichsville, OH 44683

ISBN 1-57748-615-3

TIME FOR A MIRACLE

Cover illustration by Lauraine Bush.

prologue

Wisconsin, 1880

Wind soughed through pine boughs and clattered through oak branches. Although the predawn sky was clear and starry, snow flurried, blown from scattered drifts. A lone horse and rider slogged along a path beneath the trees. Massive shoulders hunched against the cold, hat pulled over his ears, the man repeatedly glanced backward. His horse jerked its head and jigged.

With a yank on the reins, the man grumbled aloud, "Things was going so good. Now I'm back to running, always running. It ain't a fittin' life for a decent man. I never hurt nobody. I don't deserve this."

Tensing, he reined in his horse, but the sound of hoofbeats continued. Panicked, he dug in his heels, but the gelding refused to give him even a short burst of speed. Dropping its head, it took the bit between its teeth and settled into a jolting trot. The large rider berated it in obscene terms; the horse only pinned back its ears.

A cry drifted between the trees, "Hey, wait!"

Instead of pausing, the rider removed his hat and began slapping his mount's hindquarters. The horse hunched its back and threatened to buck.

Out of the shadows behind appeared a horse and rider. The stranger's horse whinnied a greeting as it slowed to a walk, and the obstinate gelding answered cheerily.

"Where are you off to at this hour, Fairfield? Why use this old Indian trail when there are good roads aplenty? A person would think you were trying to hide. . .or escape."

Recognizing the jocular voice, the first rider sighed in relief. "Don't scare me like that! I thought nobody else knew about this trail."

5

"So, where are you going?" The newcomer reined his horse alongside.

"Far away as I can get. It's a long story."

"You're surely not leaving town for good?" Sarcasm tinted the query.

"There's nothing else I can do. Say, Nick, would you meet someone for me at the train today?"

"Let me guess—Mrs. Fairfield."

"How'd you know? She's the whole problem. . .or most of it."

"I should think a lonely husband would be happy to see his little woman after all these years of solitary bachelorhood. Is she a hag or only a nag?" Derision fairly dripped from Nick's words.

The runaway swore roundly. "None of your business. Just meet her for me, would you? Tell her. . .tell her I was called away on business. Tell her it was a case of mistaken identity— I'm the wrong Jerry Fairfield. It could happen."

"Sorry, but I'm not interested, Charles."

The fat man blanched and hauled his horse to a stop. "What did you say?"

"I know who you are, Charles Rufus Bolton."

"How do you. . . ? Who are you?"

"Don't know me, do you? I didn't know you either at first, but time narrowed the possibilities. Who but you would be stupid enough to build a luxurious mansion in the middle of nowhere? Think, Charles. Who would have reason to track you all over the country these twenty years?"

"Patrick," Charles whispered, aghast.

one

"How much more shall your Father which is in heaven give good things to them that ask him?" Matthew 7:11

Picking his teeth with a clean straw, Obadiah Watson leaned against the doorframe of the blacksmith's shop and watched the outside world. There was little to be seen in the sleepy town: a wagon full of children waiting before the dry goods store, two horses tethered in front of the saloon having a squealing disagreement, a pair of elderly ladies intent upon the latest gossip, a few other men lounging in doorways. Sheriff Martin sat before his office, cleaning his rifle, his chair balanced precariously on two legs. Spotting Obie, he nodded and waved.

Behind Obie, inside the smithy, a cross-looking paint mustang stood on three legs while the burly smith rasped his left hind hoof and fitted the second of his four shoes. Tossing his head, the horse cast resentful glances at Obie, first with a blue eye, then with a brown eye.

Obie ignored his horse's indignation. "Snow's melting off quick," he observed. "Spring's here to stay, I think." Tossing the straw down, he took off his woolen jacket and laid it over a stall door, then stretched his arms over his head and swung them around to work out the kinks. Suspenders strapped his baggy shirt against his body, and dungarees tucked into his high boots at the knee.

The dour blacksmith countered, "Never depend on an early spring. Almanac predicts more snow."

A high-pitched voice drifted from across the street. "Hey, Uncle Obie!"

The children in the wagon had spotted him. Obie sauntered across the empty street to chat. "Howdy, Amos. Howdy,

Benny. Good mornin', Fern. How's the little un today?" He touched Baby Daniel's dimpled arm.

Fern shifted the baby higher on her skinny knee and answered in a lofty imitation of her mother, "Well enough. He's cuttin' teeth and drools like anything."

Daniel grinned at Obie and proved his sister correct. His chubby chins glistened in the sunlight.

"He's a cheerful chap, that's certain."

"Uncle Obie, you gotta hear what I caught last Friday: two crappies, a smallmouth bass, and a trout! I cleaned 'em just the way you showed me, and Ma cooked 'em up fer us. She says I'm an expert," Amos boasted.

"Amos, Ma says you're not to call Mr. Watson 'uncle.' He's no real relation," Bennie reminded his big brother.

"Everybody calls 'im that. It don't mean nothin'." Amos shrugged off the caution.

"You'd best obey your ma." Obie's smile faded. "I don't mind what you call me as long as we're pals."

"You'd best get on afore Ma sees us talkin' with you," Fern whispered. "Pa says we can talk to you, but Ma doesn't like it, and she makes a fuss."

A shadow crossed Obie's face, then he briskly slapped the wagon's side and backed away. "Right. You take care now. I'll see ya at the fishin' hole, Amos. You're a fine baby-watcher, Miss Fern. Good morning."

When he returned, the smith was still laboring over the same hoof. Obie avoided his horse's accusing gaze. "Hiram, I'll be at the sheriff's if you need me."

"Go on ahead," Hiram huffed, glancing over one sweaty shoulder. "Jughead's always good for me. Aren't you, boy?" The mustang swung his head around and gave the blacksmith a sour look. "He'll be here waitin' for ya."

When Obie approached, Sheriff Boz Martin set his chair legs down and collected his gun and cleaning rags. "C'mon in for coffee. How you been?"

"Well enough. We got a heifer calf yesterday morning and another due anytime. How's things with you?" Obie accepted a cup of Martin's thick, noxious brew and took a chair.

Boz lowered his considerable bulk into his armchair and sighed, sounding something like a deflating bagpipe. "Slow, mighty slow. Don't know why I took this here job, anyway. Things are popping out West, and here we sit, rubbin' elbows with sodbusters." He spat toward the brass cuspidor in the corner.

"Sorry you feel that way, Boz. Don't let me hold you back if you're wanting to leave. I'm a sodbuster now, and I like it fine. My wranglin' days are past. Feel like settling in here-abouts and putting down roots. Clearing my name just doesn't seem so important anymore. I have friends here who value me for who I am, not for what I've been. That's what counts most."

Boz chuckled. "Find a little woman to feather your nest?"

Obie looked sheepish. "Not yet, but I'm lookin'."

"Best not be too particular, at your age." Boz gulped his coffee and wiped his drooping moustache on his sleeve. This moustache was the sheriff's pride—the waxed ends curled far below his jowls, and the thickness of it obscured his mouth.

Obie thoughtfully stroked his own modest moustache with one finger. "If God wants me to marry, He'll send the right woman. There must be one somewhere who'll overlook my past."

Boz gave a derisive sniff. "As though God has answered any of your prayers. You sure are slow on the uptake. Haven't you figgered out by now that He just ain't interested in over-the-hill cowpokes like us? If there even is a God, which you couldn't prove by me."

"You ready to give up our search, Boz?" Obie's gray eyes were sober, but held no blame.

"Wish I had the guts to tell you 'yes,' but I jist cain't let an ol' pard down. I'll stay on as long as you think there's hope."

"God does answer prayer. Sometimes His answer is 'wait.' I have a feeling that my waiting time is nearly over. Can't tell you why I feel that way, but I do. Maybe while God is handing blessings my way, He'll throw in a good woman and some little ones. You never know."

Boz snorted.

Obie sipped at his coffee and wondered whether his throat and stomach retained their linings—Boz's coffee made arsenic seem like a soothing balm.

A train whistle brought his eyes up to the wall clock. The train was late again.

"Gonna meet the train?"

"Might. Have nothing better to do. You coming?"

"You go on. I got paperwork to sort out."

"Thanks for the coffee." He left the cup half full.

Obie ambled toward the station, his boots squishing through mud in the road, then clopping on the boardwalks. Lifting his hat, he rubbed at his short, thinning hair, enjoying the breeze against his scalp. On a day like this, how could a man doubt the goodness of the Lord, let alone doubt His existence?

He smiled at everyone in passing. Some people returned his smile; others ignored him or gave him chilly stares. He was used to the mixed bag of reactions.

The train had already pulled in and lay waiting, spurting steam at odd intervals. On the platform, Obie purchased a *Longtree Enquirer* from a youthful hawker, tucked the paper under his arm, and leaned against a post. As he watched people climb into and out of the passenger cars, his impassive face hid a multitude of thoughts and dreams. He watched a reunited family exchanging hugs amid joyous laughter and a pair of lovers clinging together after a long separation. His moustache twitched, and a flicker of envy touched his soul.

Lord, I know that You need single men in your service, but I grow weary of working alone for You. I ask only for someone to love—someone who will love me in return. Other men find wives; why can't I?

His sad eyes scanned the female faces in the crowd. There were sweet faces, cross faces, attractive faces, homely faces, old or young faces—not one face that captured him, not one face that—

He froze. Not five feet away she stood. Her silvery blue eyes knocked him for a loop—yet it was not their beauty alone that stunned him. He felt as though he knew her, and she also seemed to recognize him.

She smiled slightly before looking away. She was searching for someone in the crowd. Evidently his had not been the face she sought. He swallowed hard and blinked.

She was the loveliest woman he had ever beheld. Clad in a blue plaid traveling suit and a plumed hat, dark hair modestly coiled at the nape of her neck, she held a bandbox in one hand and a reticule in the other. She was not slender, but neither was she plump. In Obie's opinion, her shape and size were perfect. She was not too young; he judged her age at midthirties.

Lord. . . ? but he dared not complete the question even in his thoughts. Could this woman be the immediate answer to his prayer?

Then he realized that she was not alone. A young boy and two tall girls had descended the steps behind her and now clustered near her skirts. They, too, searched the station, but did not seem to find the face they expected to see.

Though not a soul could have guessed his thoughts, Obie Watson felt his face burn. He tipped his hat down and tried to look bored. Of course, such a prize would have been snapped up long ago. Not only was she married, but she also possessed three fine children. Their father must be the happiest and proudest of men.

The family looked worried. Irritation wrinkled the lady's brow, but she sounded resigned. "It looks as though he is late, my dears. We must wait inside the station for him."

"Mama, I'm so tired," the younger of the girls complained.

"We're all tired, Eunice."

"I bet he'll never come," the older girl stated sharply. She was taller than her mother, with olive skin and great dark eyes. "I bet it was just a cruel trick."

"Beulah, that will be enough," the mother said firmly, and the girl closed her lips.

The little boy looked pale and sad, but he manfully picked up his valise and walked behind the others into the station. Since Obie could not follow them inside without being obvious, he returned to the smithy with a heavy heart.

Lord, I know You don't play cruel jokes, so what is Your purpose here? I ask for a wife and You show me the woman of my dreams. . .but she's already married. Does this mean that I should give up my dream of a woman's love? If this is Your will, Lord, I will accept it. . .under protest.

Jughead waited at the smithy's hitching rail. At sight of Obie, he nickered with fluttering nostrils. "Howdy, ol' pard." Obie rubbed the mustang's forehead, mussing his long forelock. Then he entered the shop to pay for Hiram's service.

Minutes later, the paint trotted along the road with Obie lounging in the saddle. The horse started heading toward home, but Obie directed him to the train station. Jughead argued for a moment, then gave in with a testy snort.

Obie tethered Jughead to the rail and hurried inside. Surely the tardy husband had collected his family by now, but he would check, just in case. To his surprise and undeniable pleasure, the family still occupied the row of benches near the ticket window. He was nearly on top of them when he entered the tiny room. The ladies had been nodding off, but all three popped awake at his sudden appearance. The boy slept with his head in his mother's lap.

Obie sucked in an audible breath. Blue Eyes was even more exquisite from close range.

Three pairs of eyes regarded him expectantly, and he realized that he needed to say something. . .anything. He opened his mouth, but nothing came out. Stopping to clear his throat, he hauled off his hat and said, "I was wondering if you were still here."

The lady blinked. Her lips parted, but she seemed at a loss for words.

"I mean, I wondered if you might need help. Who's supposed to pick you up?"

"I am Violet Fairfield. Do you know my husband, Jeremiah

Fairfield?" An odd intensity colored the question.

Obie barely kept his jaw from dropping. This charming family belonged to Jerry Fairfield? Jerry had never given any indication, any hint that he possessed a wife and family. *Lord, tell me it isn't true!*

She was waiting for an answer. Obie nodded, unable to speak.

Her voice sounded choked. "You do?"

"He owns the farm next to mine."

"I see." He saw her lower lip quiver. A desire to punch Fairfield on his flabby jaw flashed through Obie's mind. What had the man done to deserve a wife like this?

"We thought Father was dead, but we learned just two weeks ago that he's alive," the younger girl proclaimed.

"Eunice, hush!"

Mrs. Fairfield turned back to Obie with a touch of color in her pale cheeks.

Just then another man stepped into the station, started with surprise, and cried, "Aren't you Violet Fairfield?"

"Yes, sir, how did you—?"

He nearly pulled her off the seat with the vigor of his hand-shake, waking the little boy. "What an unexpected surprise! Jerry asked me to come pick up a package for him today; I had no idea he meant you. What a jokester!"

"Excuse me, sir—" she began, but he interrupted.

"Pardon me, I'm Nicholas Houghton, your husband's friend." He gave Obie a glance. "Move on, pal, you aren't need—" Then he did a double take, and a look of startled guilt flashed across his features. Instantly he broke into a broad smile and proclaimed, "Thanks for trying to help, Watson. I can take it from here." Turning back to Violet, he blocked Obie's view of her with his broad shoulders.

Obie sidled to one side, feeling shorter than ever. He recognized Houghton as a handsome rogue who drifted in and out of local towns, working at various jobs and keeping the saloons in business.

Violet looked bewildered. "But where is Jeremiah?"

"He only told me that he had to go out of town. It must have been important for him to miss meeting you, Mrs. Fairfield. Jerry is one lucky man!" He laughed, showing straight white teeth that contrasted handsomely with his thick side-whiskers.

Violet Fairfield's reply was chilly. "I'm sure we are pleased to meet you." She squirmed her hand out of his grip and placed both hands behind her back. "These are my children, Beulah, Eunice, and Samuel."

Since the introduction seemed to be directed toward both men, Obie smiled at the children. Samuel caught his eye, hesitated, and smiled timidly. Eunice nodded, flashing a hint of a dimple. Beulah closed her eyes and leaned against the wall.

Mr. Houghton barely acknowledged the children. "Fine family. Since Jerry wasn't sure how late he'd be, it'd be best for you to stay overnight in town. I recommend Amelia Sidwell's boardinghouse as the finest in Longtree; I've stayed there myself on occasion. Leave your luggage, please; I'll have it delivered for you. This way, ladies, and. . .boy."

Mrs. Fairfield sent Obie an entreating look. "Is this boardinghouse one *you* would recommend?"

Houghton took the lady's elbow as if affronted. "Madam, do you not trust my advice?"

"I seek only his corroboration," she said firmly, jerking her arm out of his grasp.

"You'll be comfortable at Amelia's," Obie affirmed quietly. "I'll check on you later." Though he spoke to Mrs. Fairfield, the words carried a hint of warning to Houghton.

The tall man glowered. "This way, Mrs. Fairfield," he said stiffly. "I have a hired rig out front." She laid her gloved hand on his offered arm, but cast one last glance at Obie before exiting the room.

The children followed reluctantly. "Good-bye," Eunice said. "Hope to see you again soon."

Obie returned her wave and a moment later was alone in the station. He slowly sat on the bench and leaned against the wall. Fairfield luggage surrounded his feet.

Had Jerry Fairfield deserted his family, leaving them to believe him dead? If so, the man was a bigger fool than Obie had thought.

"Hey, cowboy!"

Obie looked up. The ticket master stood in the doorway, fists on hips. "That fancy fellow told me to have all this baggage delivered to Amelia's. What does he think this is, the post office? You can turn a penny if you'll deliver it for me. Team and wagon are in the stable beside the station."

Obie accepted the job, though he had no need of money. While it wouldn't be wise to dream about Violet Fairfield, there was nothing wrong with helping a woman in need. Until Jerry arrived to take over his responsibility, Obie determined to help the Fairfield family as he believed Jesus would under the same circumstances.

Houghton's hired surrey still waited in front of Amelia Sidwell's whitewashed clapboard house when Obie arrived. He tethered the ticket master's team and began to unload luggage. Holding a bundle under each arm and a valise in each hand, he strode up the flower-bordered walkway. The front door opened magically before him, and Eunice peeked around it. "Hello!"

"Where shall I take them?" he asked, returning her smile. She was a rather plump girl, but her smile was pure sunshine.

"I'll show you. Mr. Houghton is still talking with Mama in the parlor." She led the way upstairs and opened the first door on the left. "Right in here, sir."

Beulah perched on the guest room window seat, resting her chin on one fist and staring blankly down at the flower garden beneath her window. She gave Obie a solemn nod and turned back to the window. Samuel was asleep on the biggest bed. His thin cheeks looked too pale. Obie placed the bags on the floor and sneaked out of the room. He heard no voices from the parlor although the door stood slightly ajar.

His arms loaded again, this time with a satchel, a heavy leather grip, and two hatboxes, he shoved the front door open with his foot. A deep voice stopped him in the entryway.

"Obadiah Watson, what are you doing, carryin' bags into my house?" Amelia Sidwell looked like someone's maiden aunt, all sharp angles and flat planes, and her voice could easily have belonged to a man.

"Delivering luggage," he explained, feeling sheepish. Amelia was a good sort of woman, but she invariably triggered his "flight instinct." He sidled toward the stairway.

"That Fairfield woman ain't been in town one hour, and she's already got men fallin' over themselves to he'p her out. It figures!" Amelia chuckled. "You ain't never set foot in my house afore, and look at you now! Fool man. The woman's married, you know."

Obie made his escape, and thankfully Amelia had vanished when he returned downstairs. After a third load of bags, he brought in the massive trunk. Judging by the volume of luggage, the Fairfield family intended to stay indefinitely.

Eunice met him at the door again. "Are you sure your mother wants this upstairs?" he panted, setting the brass-bound trunk on the entryway rug. "You'll likely be moving to your house as soon as your father returns to town."

Eunice looked uncertain. "Shall I ask her?"

The parlor door flew open. Violet rushed out and nearly collided with Obie. "Pardon me—oh, it's you!" Relief swept over her face. She stepped quickly around him, clutching at his sleeve. "Did. . .did you deliver our things? I didn't realize that you worked for the railroad. . ." She glanced apprehensively over Obie's shoulder as Houghton appeared in the parlor doorway.

Obie straightened to his full height, at least a head shorter than Houghton's. "I don't, ma'am, but they asked me to deliver your things. They don't generally deliver baggage." As he spoke, he glared at Houghton, communicating a silent threat.

"I'm sorry! I was under the impression that they. . . Oh, well, what do I owe you?" Violet opened her reticule with shaking fingers.

"Not a cent, ma'am. I was happy to help out. Do you want

this trunk upstairs?" Obie never took his eyes off the other man. Almost imperceptibly he inclined his head toward the front door.

Houghton's eyes narrowed and his fists clenched, but he edged toward the door.

Mrs. Fairfield looked flustered. "But I can't let you. . .I mean, this is too kind. . ."

"Consider it a service rendered as to the Lord, ma'am, and don't let it worry you."

"Yeah, little ol' Pops Watson is always doing 'good deeds.' He's kind of an institution around town." Houghton sounded as if he thought Obie belonged in an institution. He reminded Obie of a cornered stray dog, snarling, yet with its tail between its legs.

"Mr. Watson, is it? Well, perhaps I can do something for you in return someday," Mrs. Fairfield said. "It's good to know that some people are kind without expecting payment."

Nick Houghton sent her a venomous glare. Obie moved to intercept it. His hands clenched into fists. Houghton noticed, and his sneer faded.

Oblivious to the silent confrontation, Violet continued, "Oh, and please leave the trunk down here. I will ask Mrs. Sidwell to store it until someone. . .until my husband comes for us."

His broad forehead glistening, Houghton reached behind his back for the doorknob. "I've. . .uh. . .got to return that rig. I'll see you again, Mrs. Fairfield. If you need anything, send for me. I'll likely be at the Grand Hotel."

After Houghton had slithered outside, Obie excused himself. "I'll see you around, ma'am."

"Will you be at church on Sunday?" she asked, looking as though she really cared.

"I'm generally there every week." He tipped his hat to her and winked at Eunice.

Violet followed him to the door. Before he stepped outside, she touched his sleeve. "Thank you. . .for everything."

Maybe she hadn't been oblivious after all. He swallowed

hard. "Anytime, ma'am." His voice sounded like a bullfrog's croak. Violet was scarcely touching his arm, but he felt as though he had to tear himself from her in order to walk out the door. His heart filled his chest, throbbing painfully.

Later that day, riding home on Jughead, he slouched in the saddle and dreamed. Blue eyes weren't supposed to be warm and melting; not even Obie's collie dog Treat had eyes to match Violet Fairfield's in pure eloquence. The man's lips twitched as he considered his own thoughts. The lady probably wouldn't be flattered by a comparison with a dog, but it was the best he could do.

The more he tried not to think about that woman, the more she filled his mind. Every detail of her appearance, her voice, her scent, and her touch on his arm seemed branded upon his memory. Obie had never touched a woman or held one in his arms since he was a small boy being cradled by his mother. This innocent encounter with a married woman loomed large in his mind. . .and bothered his tender conscience.

Lord, why would she look at me that way? I'm no handsome gent, and I'd stake my life she's not the type of woman to flirt with a man who isn't her husband. My best guess is that she desperately needs a friend. Is that my role in Your plan? I liked my idea better, but You know best.

two

" 'For I know the thoughts that I think toward you,'
saith the Lord, 'thoughts of peace, and not of evil,
to give you an expected end.' " Jeremiah 29:11

Violet stepped to the window and pulled back the curtain. The trotting horse she had heard continued on past the gate. Would Jeremiah come? This waiting frayed her nerves. Gnawing the side of one finger, she closed her eyes and sighed. The day had already been eternally long.

Beulah rolled over in her sleep and let out a snort. Eunice snored quietly. Samuel murmured in his sleep. Violet envied their peaceful slumber. Whether Jeremiah showed up tonight or not, Violet knew she would sleep very little.

Lord, I don't have the strength for this! I'm frightened.

Moving to the side of her bed, she slowly sat down, then lay back and closed her eyes. Even though sleep was far from her, she would rest her body and her eyes. She continued to pray, *Please give me wisdom. I feel so alone. If Jeremiah is alive, it is obvious that he no longer wants me, for he has not attempted to contact me in nearly five years. If this is simply another man with the same name, I have traveled all the way from Maryland for nothing.*

Lord, despite evidence to the contrary, I cannot believe that Jeremiah is alive. My heart tells me that he is dead. . .and yet these people claim to know him. Perhaps he was injured and has lost his memory of me. Otherwise I cannot believe that he would cease to love me—not Jeremiah. I'm sure I could teach him to love me again, perhaps revive his memory.

She shook her head abruptly. *This all seems foolish. I have mourned Jeremiah and all but forgotten my love for him.*

19

There must be some mistake. No matter what comes, I stand to look foolish in the eyes of this community.

This community. . .Violet started a new line of thought. What manner of community was this, anyway? She had scarcely noticed the town during the ride from the station.

Nicholas Houghton frightened her. In the parlor that day, he had grabbed her wrist and pulled her against him before she knew what he was about. Only by shoving him off balance had she managed to escape his powerful grasp, and even then he would surely have caught her again if that kind man. . .what was his name? Watson. . .if Mr. Watson had not rescued her. Perhaps Amelia Sidwell would know Mr. Watson's first name.

Violet's lips twitched when she recalled the way he had faced down Houghton. In retrospect, the scene was rather amusing, though she did not altogether understand what had happened. For some reason, Nick Houghton feared that living portrait of a Wild West cowboy.

Violet didn't fear Mr. Watson. She had found him charming, in a rough-cut manner. Despite his diminutive size, he was altogether masculine, and she was well aware that he found her attractive. *Would I be having such thoughts if Jeremiah were really still alive?* she wondered.

※

"Come 'ere and let me give you a kiss," Hattie Thwaite commanded, and Obie dared not refuse. Bending over her bed, he let her plant a kiss on his stubbly cheek. She patted his face with age-spotted hands, and love for him glistened in her faded blue eyes. "You're an angel straight from heaven, Obie Watson, and the Lord sent ya here just for me. Now you come back and see me soon, whether you think I'm dyin' or not, you hear?"

"I'll be back, Hattie. You take care now, and try to get some sleep." Obie tenderly patted her thin arm and walked quietly from the room.

"Obie, we cain't thank you enough for coming to us. I hated to wake ya so late at night, but Doc said she mightn't last till dawn. Now Hattie looks right hearty this morning, but you're lookin' a mite peaked," Cyrus Thwaite said, escorting his guest to the door. "Go home and get some sleep, son. I fed your horse; he shoulda finished eatin' by now."

The old man looked so frail, as though a puff of wind could have knocked him down, but Obie knew better. Cyrus was a tough old codger, likely to outlive half the town. His wife, however. . .Obie feared for the feisty, cranky little lady. She suffered from chronic digestive problems, but the doctor had told him that last night's illness had involved her heart.

"I was happy to come, Cy," he smiled, squeezing a shriveled shoulder. The Thwaites had settled in Longtree back when it was a frontier town, sixty years ago. Obie could not imagine the town or the church without them. "I'm sorry Reverend Schoengard couldn't be found, but I'm always glad to sit with a pretty lady like Hattie."

"Aw, you're a minister in all but name," Cyrus scoffed. "Your Scripture reading is as fine as any in church. The minister's reading irritates her sometimes—he pauses in all the wrong places, she says. Hattie likes your deep voice—makes her feel young, she says. You're one of the few people she really likes, you know."

Obie rolled his eyes and grinned shyly. "Well, I say you'd better watch that one; she's likely to run off with me sometime."

Cyrus chuckled. "You ever need anything from us, you let me know, Obie. And thanks for the milk and butter—Hattie says your cows give pure cream, that they do."

Out at the Thwaite's barn, Obie noticed that some fence rails had splintered, so he took a few extra minutes to repair the corral. The only nails he could find were bent and rusty, but he straightened them with a few blows of the hammer and put them to use. "That oughta hold you for a while," he told Cyrus's bony old mule.

Jughead was just finishing the last wisps of hay in his manger when Obie rousted him out. The little mustang never needed to be tied up; he stood quietly while Obie bridled and saddled him. "Wish I could do more to help around here,"

Obie told him, "but Cyrus always wants to return the favor, and he has nothing left to give. Maybe I'll sneak over some night and tinker with that pump."

Jughead yawned as Obie mounted up and headed him toward home. It was contagious. Obie also yawned widely, then let go of the reins to stretch his arms over his head. "Didn't expect this to turn into an all-nighter. Al and Myles will think I did it just to get out of my chores." He smiled sleepily and picked up the reins.

A cluck and a whoop brought Jughead to life, and the paint broke into his ground-eating lope. "Let's get home, buddy."

ᔫ

"Honey, you've been staring out windows since dawn. Why don't you and the children go to church with me this morning? If Jerry got in late last night, he mighta figured it was too late to wake you and went on home." Amelia stood in the dining room doorway holding a stack of clean china plates.

"Maybe so," Violet sighed, restraining a yawn. "I would like to attend church. I'll hurry the children up. When will you leave?"

"In about twenty minutes."

"We'll be ready." Violet desperately needed some spiritual support.

ᔫ

"Are you sure you want to go to church, cousin? Thought you'd want some sleep after sitting up all night. Go ahead, if that's what you want. Myles and I can take care of things here. Marigold delivered this little fellow at the crack of dawn with no trouble. She didn't miss you, far as I could tell." Al grinned at Obie while rubbing the Jersey cow at the base of her horns. The gentle animal leaned into the boy's caresses.

Albert Moore, Obie's young cousin, had traveled east from California with him four years earlier. Along with Myles Trent, their hired man, the two had turned their farm into a prosperous operation through hard work and sensible investments. They had differences of opinion about how the farm should be run, but usually resolved these without any hard feelings.

Obie hovered uncertainly in the barn doorway. "It's a fine calf, Al—every bit the Jersey bull we'd hoped for. But. . .are you sure you don't mind me running off?"

"Not now that the milking's done. You go on. I'll have a private time with the Lord later today. He won't mind me missing church this once. Get going, or you'll be late."

Obie headed outside, picking his way between mud puddles. It was a brilliant morning, though the air was still chilly. Jughead waited at the hitching rail, his long ears pricked. Spotting Obie, he gave a cheerful nicker.

"You're a pal, Jughead," Obie answered. "Ready for church?" He swung into the saddle and turned the horse toward town.

Obie had changed into a blue-gray wool shirt and black wool trousers that bagged around his hips. The clothes were hot and itchy, but he wanted to look his best. His boots were polished, and his string tie sported a silver concho. He smelled clean after a quick morning sponge bath.

He pushed Jughead into a lope, enjoying the breeze on his face. Soon, town buildings appeared on the horizon and the church steeple came into sight. Horses and assorted vehicles already crowded the yard, and the church building bustled with people.

Reverend David Schoengard delivered a stirring sermon about the building of Solomon's temple, but Obie heard little of the message. He sat in the back of the church, arms folded across his chest, and studied the back of Violet's hat. She sat at one end of a row with Amelia Sidwell on the far end and the three children in between.

After the service, a few people clustered at the end of Violet's pew to introduce themselves and welcome her. When she lifted her face to greet them, Obie noted the pallor of her smooth cheeks and the dark circles beneath her eyes. Then Obie saw Caroline Schoengard, the pastor's wife, greet Violet in her friendly way, and he relaxed his vigil. Perhaps Violet would not need his friendship after all.

Samuel caught sight of Obie, tugged Eunice's sleeve, and

pointed him out to her. Obie winked and waved, and the two children brightened. As Beulah talked with another girl her age, her moody look faded away. She was rather handsome when she smiled.

The congregation gradually moved outside, and Obie drifted with the flow, keeping the Fairfields in sight. His distracted air puzzled friends who spoke to him, for Obie was usually an attentive listener. The Fairfield family moved toward Amelia's surrey as though preparing to leave. Obie wavered. He wanted to speak with Violet, yet he had no good reason to detain her.

"Uncle Obie, sir, my brothers want to ask you for a ride."

Glancing down and back, Obie smiled at a six-year-old with serious blue eyes and wild yellow hair. "They do, eh?"

Four-year-old twins held hands and nodded in unison. One popped a finger into his mouth. "Good morning, Scott, Bernie, Ernie. Does your mother know where you are?"

All three boys nodded again. Unable to resist their pleading eyes, Obie followed them to a grassy place alongside the church. It was just as well. For his own sake, he needed to forget about Violet Fairfield. As soon as Obie bent down, Reverend Schoengard's three sons tackled him, and he rolled over, laughing. Other children came running from all directions to join in the fun.

☙

An elderly gentleman with a ring of silvery hair around the back of his head was just pulling the door shut, preparing to lock it, when Violet clattered up the church steps.

"Excuse me, sir! I left my Bible inside."

"Now that be one possession a body cain't do without fer a week," the kindly man said, opening the door for her. "We're almighty glad you joined us today, Miz Fairfield."

Violet walked quickly to the correct row, picked up her worn Bible, and hurried back outside. "Thank you, sir. I'm afraid I don't recall your name. . . ?"

"Jes' call me Cyrus, ma'am. I'm sort of the trustee of this here church building. My wife isn't well today—"

A female voice spoke at Violet's elbow. "It's good to finally have you here, Mrs. Fairfield. Most of us were unaware until recently that Mr. Fairfield was married. Since he never attends church, it's a pleasure to find that you, at least, seek fellowship with God's people."

Cyrus murmured a farewell and slipped quietly down the steps.

My Jeremiah always attended church. Violet's doubts waxed stronger. She mustered a polite smile. "We are pleased to be here, Mrs. . . ?"

"Leila Blackthorn." The plump woman bounced a smiling baby on her hip. Her own face looked as though it would crack if she were to venture a smile.

"Mrs. Blackthorn. Thank you for your gracious welcome. You have a sweet boy there," she indicated the baby.

"He's my fourth."

Hoping to cut the conversation short, Violet descended the steep church stairs while shading her eyes with one hand. "This sunshine is amazingly bright."

"The mud will vanish soon; that's a mercy," Mrs. Blackthorn concurred. "It was an early spring this year. I must say, Mrs. Fairfield, you seem a genteel woman, though I disapprove of lip rouge. A virtuous woman shouldn't paint her face, in my opinion. It gives the wrong impression to men."

"I beg your pardon. I do not paint my face."

"Indeed!" Mrs. Blackthorn lifted a doubtful brow. "Isn't that gown rather thin and flimsy for a married woman of your age? Puffed sleeves and no bustle or train? Hmpf!"

"Bustles are not presently in style back East. This gown is fashioned in the aesthetic style, which is known to be good for the health." Violet resisted the urge to stick her nose in the air, but it wasn't easy.

Mrs. Blackthorn seemed to be searching for a scathing put-down, but just as the two women reached the bottom step, a scream of childish laughter pierced their ears, and a man crawled past on all fours with a little boy perched upon his back. "Faster, faster, mustang!" the small wrangler commanded, wriggling to spur his mount on to greater speed. A cluster of laughing children scampered behind, shouting encouragement. A deep chuckle occasionally joined the shrill giggles and squeals.

Violet recognized that voice, and a smile softened her lips. Obie Watson reared up and pawed the air like an outlaw horse, carefully placing one hand behind the child to keep him secure.

"Amos! Fern! Get to the wagon at once," Mrs. Blackthorn screeched. Two of the children stopped, sent their mother horrified glances, and ran like rabbits toward the parking area.

"Disgraceful behavior," the woman whispered to Violet, enraged. "On the Lord's Day, and at the Lord's house! I must speak with the pastor. His wife allows his children to associate with absolutely *anyone*. They are leading my own children down the path of iniquity, playing with that. . .that felon! All I can say is, Reverend Schoengard shall rue the day."

"I enjoy watching children play any day of the week. I don't believe the Lord disapproves of his people having fun," Violet defended both Obie and the pastor's wife. Caroline Schoengard had given her a warm welcome—she did not care to hear the woman maligned. And what did Mrs. Blackthorn mean by calling Mr. Watson a felon?

"Well, I never!" After raking Violet with a scathing glare, Leila Blackthorn hitched up the baby and stalked away.

Although Violet knew Amelia and the children were waiting, she could not resist pausing to watch the horseplay for a moment. Her tension seemed to melt away as she watched the man romp with the little children. What an endearing sight! She strolled closer.

The little rider's clutching hands covered his "horse's" eyes, directing Obie with voice commands. "Faster! Turn left! Rear up!" Obie crawled on, waggling his head like a real horse. The other children laughed at the sight and shouted their own commands. Violet was pleased when they moved closer until, amid all the noise, Obie turned abruptly and charged into her skirts. The top of his head bumped into the side of her knee, and the little rider nearly disappeared amid blue bombazine ruffles.

"Oh!" she cried, taking two quick steps back. Embarrassed, she didn't immediately see the humor in the situation.

Little Ernie Schoengard stared up at her, and the other children backed hastily away, then turned and ran for their mothers. Too late, Ernie uncovered Obie's eyes, scrambled down, and followed his brothers.

Violet watched Obie's eyes slowly move up her figure until they met her gaze. "Good day, Mr. Watson." She resisted the urge to rub her aching knee.

"Mrs. Fairfield, I'm so sorry!" Hastily he rose, beating at his woolen trousers. It was a hopeless endeavor. Grass stains darkened the knees. His long boots, shirt, and suspenders were damp. He reached up for his hat, but he wasn't wearing one. "How are you this morning?"

"You're forgiven, and I'm well enough, thank you. It was my fault for standing too close to your riding arena, anyway." She extended her gloved hand. "It's good to see you again."

For a moment he stared at her hand, then his own hand lifted to touch it. His heavy leather glove was caked with drying mud. She saw him notice the dirt, then whip off the glove and grip her hand firmly in his bare hand. It felt hot and rough with calluses that snagged her delicate gloves.

"Yes, it is good." His voice was soft, yet so deep that it seemed to reverberate somewhere within her soul. When he released her hand, she felt bereft. These unfamiliar emotions disturbed her.

"I suppose you've heard that Mr. Fairfield has not yet come home. I don't know what to do. . . . No one can possibly understand this. . .situation, and I feel so alone. . . ."

Intense gray eyes flashed up to search hers. Startled, she lifted a hand to still her suddenly pounding heart. Blood rushed to her cheeks.

"I. . .oh! I'm sorry to babble on so. . ."

His moustache lifted ever so slightly at the corners, and he said, "If you need help, ma'am, I'll be around."

"I appreciate your offer, Mr. Watson." Violet heard her voice quiver. She sounded like a lovesick girl!

He walked her back to Amelia's surrey and supported her elbow while she climbed up. When seated, she turned to thank him. He nodded to her and Amelia, then strode away. Although he had a slightly rolling gait, his legs were straight, not bowed. He walked with head high and shoulders square, a man of confidence.

Violet realized that she was holding her breath. Glancing at Amelia, she intercepted a speculative stare.

"Amelia, what do you think of Mr. Watson?" she asked.

"Obadiah is a good man. He and his cousin work a farm next to your husband's place."

"Obadiah." Violet considered the name. "He has the kindest eyes I've ever seen."

Amelia gave her a sober glance. "How long you been married, Miz Fairfield?"

"I married Jeremiah nineteen years ago—just before he left for war. He was several years my senior, but always seemed younger somehow. You. . .you know him, don't you?"

"I've seen him about."

"Beulah has his eyes and coloring, and Eunice has his dimples. Samuel looks more like my family, especially my father."

Amelia glanced back at the children, then gave Violet another odd look. "Do tell."

"What do you think of Mr. Houghton?"

Amelia snorted. "Now there's a feller I'd keep my gals away from, iffen I was you."

"My opinion exactly. He's very good-looking, but I don't trust him an inch. Now Obadiah Watson strikes me as an honest, trustworthy man. You say he's a farmer? He looks like a cowboy to me. Maybe it's the boots or the hat."

Amelia studied her guest with sympathetic eyes. "Honey, I do my best to mind my own business and not hand out unwanted advice, but I'd say you need to borrow this rig of mine and drive out to your house today."

"On Sunday?"

"Why ever not? Lots of people take a drive on Sunday afternoon. It don't seem to bother the Lord none. Iffen your husband is at the house, he may be wondering why you haven't come a-lookin' for him."

Violet nodded. "Perhaps you're right. We'll eat dinner first, then drive out. . .if you'll draw me a map. I'm dreadful with directions."

As they turned the corner to her street, Amelia snapped, "Well, look who's a-waitin' for us. Don't be too uppity right off; maybe he's got news about your man."

Nicholas Houghton waited on the boardinghouse porch. He grinned and waved as the surrey pulled into the drive. "Good day, Violet!"

Violet returned his wave. "Please don't leave us alone together, Mrs. Sidwell!" she pleaded, awkwardly climbing down over the surrey's wheel before Houghton could reach her. Her dress caught on a protruding bolt, but she released it undamaged. The children easily jumped down from the rear seat.

Amelia nodded. "Let me turn the team over to the stable-boy, and I'll be right in to join you."

Nick hurried up the path with an outstretched hand, chiding, "Violet, next time wait for me to assist you down. You might have fallen. Ah, my dear, you are well named, for your face is truly like a flower—refreshing to my eyes. Has Jerry not yet come to claim his bride?" As they stepped inside, he glanced around the entryway as though expecting Violet's husband to pop out of a corner.

"I hoped you had come with news of him."

Violet turned to the children. "Go on and change into play-clothes. We'll be leaving after dinner."

"I haven't seen Jerry since yesterday. Perhaps he was delayed. May I treat you to supper at the hotel tonight? Amelia is an excellent cook, but I think you would appreciate our hotel's fine cuisine." Taking her arm, Houghton drew Violet into the parlor, leaving the door slightly ajar.

"I don't believe Jeremiah would like that, sir. What if he were to come while I was away?"

"Ah, Violet, let us speak honestly, as adult man to adult woman. We both know that Jeremiah Fairfield has not been the husband a woman like you deserves," Nick murmured, letting his blue eyes drift over her face and body. "I cannot believe that he would leave you alone for so many years. The man must be blind as well as. . . Surely you have learned, during that time, to find solace in the company of other men."

"You are mistaken, sir!" Violet cried, aghast. "You know nothing of me if you believe such rubbish—and my husband was very good to me."

"I hope you don't believe that he has pined for you all these years," Houghton scoffed. "If so, you're a bigger fool than—"

Amelia entered the room, wielding a feather duster. "Don't mind me," she assured them. "Just touchin' up a bit before Mr. Fairfield arrives."

Muscles worked in Houghton's jaw, making his whiskers twitch, but he forced a smile and changed the subject. His intensely blue eyes studied Violet even as he spoke of trivial town gossip. She disliked him more with each passing minute. Oddly enough, he seemed confident that she found him attractive.

When he finally rose to take his leave, he pulled Violet aside and whispered fiercely, "Where can we meet to speak privately? Somewhere *she* won't be." He jerked a thumb in Amelia's direction. "It's important for your future, Violet."

Violet was skeptical about the importance of his message, but she replied, "I don't know at present. Ask me another time."

As soon as they had eaten, Violet loaded up her children and headed into the countryside, armed with a scrawled map. Amelia had scoffed at the idea of getting lost. "Jist look for a house the size of a castle, and you'll find it soon enough. Iffen ya do get lost, ask directions at any house along the road. Everyone knows Fairfield's Folly."

Last night's snow had vanished. The road was muddy and

rutted, but someone had filled in the worst of the ruts with gravel. Nervous though she was, Violet enjoyed the delightful scenery. Feathery clouds drifted across a sky bluer than Nick Houghton's eyes. Trees rustled tiny new leaves in a cool breeze.

Samuel exclaimed, "Look, there's a fox!" and "I just saw a cardinal! Did you see it?"

The girls seemed indifferent at first, but soon their interest was caught. "There is a vireo, I'm absolutely certain," Beulah stated, trying to hide her excitement. "And that yellow bird was a warbler."

"I think it was a goldfinch," Eunice disagreed.

"It was beautiful, whatever it was." Violet tried to avert an argument. "Isn't this lovely country?"

"Oh, Mama, I had no idea!" Eunice raved. "When Father talked about going west to farm, I somehow imagined flat grassland or desert."

"We're not that far west," Violet explained. "This is west of Maryland, for certain, but we are a long way from the Wild West. They call this region the Midwest, I believe."

"Mama, this must be our turn. There's the white barn Miss Sidwell mentioned." Beulah pointed out the landmark.

Her heart thumping with apprehension, Violet obediently directed the horses up a neat driveway. The drive led to a farm with a low-slung log house and a large red barn. Several golden-brown cows stopped grazing to watch the buggy pass their pasture.

"This can't be right," Violet groaned. "But I guess we can ask for directions, like Amelia said."

Obadiah Watson emerged from an outbuilding, brushing his hands on a huge leather apron. Violet's heart thudded in startled recognition. "May I help you, Mrs. Fairfield?"

"I believe we are lost, Mr. Watson. Can you direct us to our farm? Amelia Sidwell told me to turn right when I saw a white barn on my left."

"Yes, but your drive is about a hundred yards beyond ours. Head west on the main road and look for a path through the trees. It's easy to miss, even when you know what you're looking for."

Violet didn't intend to look helpless and pleading—at least not consciously. But she was relieved when Watson abruptly said, "I'll ride with you a ways and make sure you find it. Wait a moment, please."

"What will Father say?" Eunice murmured as Obie emerged from the barn. He wore a flat-brimmed hat and had removed the leather coverall.

Violet tried to shrug off her concern. "I'm sure he would understand. Besides, if your father had come for us, this wouldn't be necessary."

She scooted over to make room, but Obie did not immediately climb up. "We delivered a calf this morning before church. Perhaps the children would like to see it?"

"Oh, could we?" Eunice said eagerly, and Samuel laid a beseeching hand on his mother's shoulder.

"Very well. If you don't mind waiting, Mr. Watson, I certainly don't."

Samuel scrambled down over the surrey's tall wheel. This time Violet was willing to accept help. To her surprise, Obie grasped her by the waist and lifted her bodily down. Hands upon his shoulders, she met his eyes, and color tinged her pale cheeks. "Thank you, Mr. Watson."

Inside the barn, Obie called, "Al? Myles? We have visitors to see the calves."

Two men came to meet the unexpected company. The younger man had straight black hair and dark eyes. The older man was ruddy of hair, beard, and skin.

"I'm sorry to disturb you. We lost our way, and Mr. Watson has offered to show us the new calf before he puts us back on the right track. I am Violet Fairfield, and these are my children, Beulah, Eunice, and Samuel."

Both men bowed politely, murmuring greetings. Al was a handsome boy with smiling eyes. "Ma'am, I've heard so much about you."

"Have you?" Violet asked, not knowing what else to say.

Had Obie told him about her? Or perhaps Jeremiah?

"Where's the calf?" Samuel blurted impatiently.

"Right this way," Al directed, leading them to a stall. A cow stood in the roomy box stall with her head half-buried in a manger full of fresh hay. A small bundle lay beside her, knobby legs folded haphazardly.

Violet took one look at the calf's liquid eyes and melted. "Oh, isn't she sweet? Like a tiny fawn."

"He," Al corrected with another grin. "It's a bull calf."

"What's his name?" Samuel asked.

The calf gave an abrupt "Moo" and struggled to its feet.

"He doesn't have one yet."

"I would call him 'Moo-moo.' "

Obie and Al exchanged an amused smile.

Since the calf was so new, they took only a quick look at him; but the heifer calf in the next stall was active and curious about the visitors. Although the mother cow looked grouchy, she only lowed and shook her head.

"Hollyhock calved the day before yesterday. We leave the calves with their mothers for a few days before weaning them to a pail." Al seemed to have taken over their tour. Myles had disappeared, and Obie hovered in the background.

Leaning over the Dutch door, Beulah crooned at the dainty calf, rubbing its bristly forehead. "Does she have a name?"

Obie suddenly coughed, and Violet turned just in time to see him shake his head, eyes intent upon Al. Al coughed in return, and Violet suspected him of hiding a smile. "All of our cows are named for flowers. What would *you* call her?" Al parried the question.

"Rosebud," Beulah answered without hesitation.

"We already have a Rosie," Al said apologetically. "But it is a pretty name, you're right. She's a fine calf."

Next he led them to a box stall containing a dozing red sow with a large litter of squealing piglets. Eunice and Samuel were delighted when Al escorted them into the stall and handed them each a pig, but Beulah went back to the tiny heifer. She found pigs repulsive. Violet was thankful when the mother pig paid no attention to the squalls of her offspring.

"Brunhilda trusts me," Al explained, interpreting Violet's nervous glances at the immense sow.

"Brunhilda?" Violet smiled. "Does she sing opera?"

"An aria now and then." Obie's deep voice at her side made Violet jump. He leaned his elbows on the door beside her.

She felt slightly giddy. "I'm not sure I want to hear one. Is she a soprano?"

"Brunhilda sings parts from bass to high soprano—sometimes all at once." Obie's eyes twinkled. "She's Al's project. I don't care much for hogs."

Al spoke up, "Cousin Buck wants to specialize in dairy cattle. He wants to build a silo so we can keep more cows over the winter. I like a variety of animals and crops."

"And since you do most of the work around here, that's what we've got," Obie added.

Violet glanced at Obie, intending to ask the identity of "Buck"; but when she discovered that Obie was looking at her children and not at her, she took the opportunity to examine him.

Obadiah Watson was only three or four inches taller than Violet's five-foot-two, so she didn't have to tip her head back to look at his face—a pleasant change for her. His top several shirt buttons were undone, displaying the neckline of his red woolen combinations. His jaw and neck were neatly shaven, and he looked and smelled clean. His moustache and hair were salt-and-pepper gray, though his eyebrows were black. Smile lines creased his tanned face.

"How often must you milk the cows?" she asked, picturing him at the chore.

"Twice a day."

"I've never milked a cow. I would like to learn how. Does. . . my husband raise cattle?"

"No, ma'am." Obie opened one of his hands, turning it over. The back of it was leathery and hairy; two of the knuckles had abrasions and the palm was calloused. It was the hand of a man who worked hard for a living. "Milking takes strong hands and a strong back."

"Do you think I'm too weak to do it?" Violet asked. For some reason, she felt concerned about the possibility of failure in his eyes.

"Lots of women milk cows."

Violet met his smiling eyes and felt her heart grow warm. Obadiah Watson was not flirting with her, she knew. With him she felt...safe.

Al took the piglets from the children and returned them to their mother. Obie unlatched the stall door, and Samuel and Eunice exited, dirty but happy. Al stayed behind to care for Brunhilda and her progeny.

There was a tug at Obie's sleeve. "Do you own any dogs, Mr. Watson?"

Samuel's quiet inquiry captured Obie's attention. He smiled at the boy, deepening every one of those creases on his face. "Not only do we own a dog, she just had pups. This farm is overrun with babies."

"May I see them?"

Obie glanced at Violet, seeking her approval. Though Violet had a premonition that she would be hearing more about these pups in the near future, she nodded. Obie led the boy to a storage room, and Violet trailed along behind. For a short man, Obie had a long, rapid stride.

"Treat?" he called softly at the open doorway. "Visitors to see your family." He explained as they entered, "Usually Treat woulda been first to greet you, but today she's busy. Her pups were born a week ago."

Sliding into the limited space, Obie closed the door behind Violet. A small window lighted the room, revealing neat wooden bins along the back wall. A wooden crate filled with wood shavings took up much of the floor space. Inside it, a black collie-type dog lay curled protectively around four pups. She growled softly as they entered, although her white-tipped tail wagged.

"Easy, girl," Obie soothed. "These are friends."

Crowded in the small space near the door, Obie and Violet

watched Samuel kneel beside the box and admire the nursing pups. "Your children are beautiful, Treat," he assured the watchful mother. "I would never harm them. I'm your friend Samuel."

Treat's ears lifted for a moment, and her almond eyes studied the boy. Then she yawned widely and lay back, lifting a white foreleg to offer more of her furry belly to the pups. She had accepted Samuel in a matter of moments.

Violet looked at Obie and met his meaningful gaze. She gave a little nod, then a rueful shrug. A puppy would be a wonderful companion while Samuel adjusted to his new home, but Violet would have to speak with Jeremiah before allowing the boy a pet. Obie nodded agreement, as if he'd understood her thoughts.

Perhaps her special feeling for this man was the beginning of a wonderful friendship. On that thought, she smiled at Obie, and his face lit up in response.

Yes, this would be a special friendship indeed.

three

*"So are the ways of every one that is greedy of gain;
which taketh away the life of the owners thereof."*
Proverbs 1:19

"Thank you for taking time to show us your animals." Violet extended her hand to Al, and he shook it bashfully.

"You're surely welcome, ma'am. Drop by anytime you like."

While Al assisted the girls and Samuel into the surrey's rear seat, Obie helped Violet up and over the front wheel. She liked his touch, but she felt uneasy about her reaction. It felt strangely right when he climbed up beside her and took the reins, which she was happy to relinquish. Old Brownie and Ted were not difficult to handle, but Violet had never liked to drive.

"I learned a lot about farming today. Your cattle are pretty animals. I had never seen a pretty cow before. My father kept one, but she was ugly. I always liked her, though," she amended, hoping Obie would not be offended by her criticism of a long-dead milk cow.

Slowly he turned to look at her, and she saw amusement in his eyes—not mockery, but a twinkle that brought a responsive smile to her lips. "I'm so glad to hear that you liked a cow."

Before Violet could think of an answer, Obie made a right turn into a shady vale and slowed the team to a walk. Wagon tracks seemed to run directly into a stand of trees, but as they approached, the trees gave way. Tall weeds brushed against the surrey's undercarriage as it jounced over ruts and splashed through potholes. Violet held on with both hands, but she bumped against Obie more than once. Branches reached to scratch and claw at the surrey's fringed top, even snatching at Violet's hat.

Obie apologized, "I'm sorry. I didn't expect the drive to be so rough." Hauling the horses to a stop, he indicated, "Here's your house."

"Oh!" Violet gasped, unconsciously clutching Obie's arm. He looked down at her hands, then up at her startled face.

There was a chorus of gasps and sighs from the children.

It was a tall house, framed by several flowering fruit trees. Ornate grillwork and moldings decorated each gable, and many glass windows sparkled in the bright sunlight. A wide veranda wrapped around the front; Violet immediately imagined it replete with rocking chairs and dozing cats.

"Mama, is this really our house?" Beulah cried from the rear seat. "It's magnificent!"

"It's enormous!" Eunice exclaimed.

"Is that a crick over there?" Samuel blurted.

"Sure enough," Obie assured him, and clucked the team back into motion. "Mr. Fairfield had the house designed and built by a fellow from Madison. I imagine he had it built with you all in mind."

Violet looked puzzled. "I had no idea that farming was such a. . .a lucrative career." Absently she released Obie's arm and retied the ribbons of her bonnet. The house looked empty, but perhaps Jeremiah was sleeping inside after a long night on the road. The very thought of it shook her up. She felt jumpy and irritable.

Now Obie looked puzzled. "Lucrative? Farming? I should say not. Not around here, anyway. I thought your husband was independently wealthy. He purchased the farm, but never bothered to work it much."

Violet turned on her seat to stare at Obie. "Jeremiah went west to try farming, but he had little money. I assumed that he homesteaded land here, you know, lived on it and worked it for a certain amount of time until it became his. Isn't that how it's done?"

"Not around here," he repeated.

They stared at each other, pondering the situation. "I imagine your husband will answer your questions when you see him," Obie finally concluded.

Violet shook her head doubtfully. She tried to be calm, but her heart raced and her knees quaked beneath her gown. When they stopped at the hitching rail and Obie lifted her down, she had a sudden desire to bury her face in his shoulder and hide from the future. A fog seemed to envelop her, a dread of. . .something she could not place. Not of Jeremiah, certainly. Never could she have dreaded her dear husband, but her heart told her clearly that Jeremiah was nowhere near. Only pride enabled her to release her hold on Obie's supportive arm and stand alone.

The children hopped down without help, and Samuel set out to explore. "Don't go into the woods, dear," Violet called before he disappeared around the back of the house.

"I won't" floated back to her ears.

Resolutely, Violet lifted her skirts, climbed the steps, and rapped the ornate brass knocker. While waiting, she studied the veranda. In other circumstances she would have been thrilled with this house.

"Are you sure this is our father's house?" Beulah quizzed Obie. "It doesn't look like something Father would build."

"Quite sure," he stated flatly. "Guess I'll walk on home now." Heading down the short flagstone walkway, he turned back to say, "If you need anything, our farm is due east across the creek."

Violet panicked. Obie seemed like the one solid, dependable person connected with her present state of affairs. "I have no key. If he's not here, how will we get inside?" She cast another helpless look at her unlikely knight-errant.

"He might hide a key somewhere. Just a moment, I'll look around back." Obie jogged to the back of the house. Then they heard him call sharply, "Mrs. Fairfield?"

Violet and her daughters exchanged looks. In single file they trotted back down the steps and around the house.

Obie waited at a side door, his face sober. The glass panes were shattered, and the door stood ajar. "Oh, my!" Violet covered her mouth with one hand.

"Ma'am, let me check inside first," he requested.

Violet looked into his grave eyes and nodded helplessly. "Please do." She put her arms around her daughters while they waited for Obie to return. "Let's pray, girls. We need wisdom to know what to do."

"I like Mr. Watson, Mama," Eunice said quietly. "Do you?"

"Yes, dear. I like him very much. I think God sent him to help us right now."

The three bowed their heads while Violet spoke a simple request for guidance.

When they lifted their heads, Beulah said, "Mama, you don't think Father is really alive. I can tell that you don't, and I don't either. I think we're entering a stranger's house uninvited. I think God lost control somehow, and our world has gone crazy—that's what I think."

"I am confused, Beulah. But I know a few things for certain: God has not lost control, God loves us, and He has a plan in all of this. We just can't see it right now."

The girls still looked worried.

Obie appeared in the doorway. "Your husband isn't here. Somebody ransacked the house."

Violet released her breath in a puff. A thief had broken in, that was all.

Obie stepped back to allow them entrance into a large kitchen with a modern cookstove and a pump at the sink. Cupboard doors hung open; cans and utensils littered the floor. The table was ugly, the chairs mismatched, but the room itself was handsome. "It's got newfangled gadgets I'd never heard of before," Obie commented, trying the pump handle. "This one seems mighty practical."

"Imagine, running water inside the house!" Eunice exulted.

Violet led the way from room to room. The hardwood flooring amplified their footsteps. "How beautiful!" Violet breathed. In spite of shredded chair cushions, fireplace ashes, and andirons scattered across the floors, the house was fine indeed. A fieldstone fireplace dominated the sitting room; a carved balustrade accented the stairway. A crystal chandelier hung in the dining room, looking lonely in the otherwise empty chamber. Plasterwork decorated the downstairs ceilings and moldings, making each room a separate work of art.

"The damage could be easily repaired," Violet remarked, picking up a shard of pottery. "Isn't this house magnificent?"

The girls agreed heartily, but Obie muttered, "Too busy by half."

While Obie opened a window to let in fresh air, the girls and their mother began to peer inside closets and cupboards. "Mama, this is the nicest house ever," Eunice proclaimed. "I love it! Have you ever seen so many closets in all your life?"

"I'll be first upstairs!" Beulah announced, and clattered up the wooden steps. "I do believe there's a closet in every room up here," she called down the stairwell. "And what a glorious view! Mama, there's a small lake not too far away. I surely do wish this house were ours."

Violet and Eunice followed, hurrying from room to room. Each of the four large bedrooms did boast a window and a commodious closet.

Entering the master bedroom, Violet stopped short, her eyes wide. A bow-tie quilt she had stitched with her own hands many years earlier lay in tatters across a shredded bolster.

Trembling, she crossed the room and lifted the window sash. Feather-tick stuffing drifted up from the slashed mattress as she gazed sightlessly out the window. *Am I wrong, Lord? Is Jeremiah alive?* Even as she prayed, she shook her head. Despite the quilt, this room felt like a stranger's bedroom.

Attempting to shrug off her apprehension, Violet hurried to find the girls. "Perhaps we can return in the morning and begin cleaning up the house. If. . .*when* your father comes, I will discuss with him the possibility of sending for our furniture—the things that belonged to your grandparents. Since we have this lovely house, we should fill it with the beautiful things we already own rather than order new ones."

"I want to stay here always, Mama," Eunice declared. Elbows on the windowsill of a back bedroom, she stared into the forest beyond the barn. "I want this bedroom, all right? This place feels like home."

୬

Obie found Samuel squatting beside a limpid pool just above a beaver dam. He sat beside the boy, gazing into the brown depths. A sleek form swished past, leaving ripples upon the surface.

"This pond is full of trout," the man observed quietly. "Some of the local boys use it as their fishin' hole."

"I can hardly wait to drop a line in there. I wonder if Father ever fishes here."

"He might."

"Do you fish here?"

"I've caught a string or two. My farm begins on the far bank, so we share the pool and this stretch of the crick. Beavers made this pond. Their house is over there in the deepest part."

"I saw trees they had chewed."

"Didn't your mother tell you to stay out of the forest?"

"This isn't the forest, it's just a stone's throw from the springhouse." Samuel looked anxious, but Obie nodded, apparently satisfied with the explanation.

"Is Father in the house?"

"No, he isn't here."

Samuel appeared neither disappointed nor relieved. "I barely remember him. I was pretty little when he left us. I remember his dark eyes and bushy black side-whiskers, but that's about all."

Obie gave the boy a quick glance and frowned. Samuel's description did not match the Jerry Fairfield he knew. Could there be some mistake, or was the child's memory faulty?

Boy and man sat quietly for long minutes, content to watch flitting damselflies and listen to birdcalls. A plunk sounded across the pool, and a V-shaped ripple in the water indicated a beaver's path. Obie and Samuel exchanged glances and smiled.

Approaching from behind, Violet saw them share that smile, and her heart warmed. Samuel rarely smiled. Obie

Watson was good medicine for the boy, it seemed.

"I hate to interrupt, but we need to be getting on back to town. I must return Amelia's surrey."

The man rose quickly, brushing off his backside. "Then I'll be getting on home now." He held aside branches for Violet and followed her back to the house. Samuel reluctantly trailed behind.

Brownie and Ted, waiting at the rail, suddenly lifted their heads and whinnied. An answer came from the direction of the road. Moments later a riderless horse trudged down the drive, limping painfully. It was saddled, and its reins dangled loose.

Obie approached it, talking softly to the large liver-chestnut horse. The animal was skittish at first, but he calmed under Obie's firm, gentle hands. Obie felt its shoulders and legs and checked it over thoroughly.

He turned to Violet, and she quailed at the expression in his eyes. "Mrs. Fairfield, this is Jerry's horse, Barabbas."

"Do you. . .do you think maybe the horse fell with Jeremiah? Is that why it limps?"

"Maybe, but I don't think so. One rein is snapped short, so I'd guess that Barabbas stepped on it and lamed himself when he was coming home alone. One way or another, it doesn't look good. I'll tell the sheriff right away, and we'll go looking for Jerry."

Violet felt weak. "If you think it's necessary. . . ," she faltered. "Mr. Watson, you have been very kind to us. Thank you for all you've done."

He did not seem to know how to respond, but Violet thought his color heightened.

Impulsively she said, "I would like to go with you on your search."

He lifted a brow. "Why?"

"Well, because this man may be my husband."

She saw a flicker in his eyes. "You have doubts, then?" Abruptly his voice changed, grew harsher. "You watch over your younguns and leave this to men." He took her elbow and directed her toward the surrey.

Violet bristled. "Are you implying that I would be in the way?" She glared down at him as he helped her to the seat.

Still grasping her arm, he said, "I'm not implyin' anything. I'll tell you straight out—you'd be in the way. You don't know the area, and I reckon you don't ride any better than you drive." Obie's eyes sparked with a blend of amusement and irritation as he backed away. "You'd be nothin' more than a distraction."

Violet flushed, angry, but lacking a snappy rejoinder. "I have a right to search for my own husband." Now she argued simply for the principle of the thing.

Obie loosed the team, settled the reins in her hands, and handed her the whip.

"Then you'll search alone, 'cause you aren't comin' with me." Turning on his heel, he left her gasping like a landed trout.

❧

When Violet drove into Amelia's yard, Nicholas Houghton appeared in the stable doorway. "Where have you been? I've been looking everywhere for you, and that Sidwell witch wouldn't tell me a thing."

While the children scrambled down from the surrey, Violet had no choice but to let Nick lift her down. His grip felt intimate, disrespectful. She released herself quickly. "I've been to our house."

"Alone?"

Violet turned the team and rig over to Amelia's stableboy, telling him, "Thank you very much."

"Violet, did you drive out to that house alone?" Nick persisted.

"If you call the four of us alone, then yes." Violet marched toward the house, removing her gloves. Nick trailed after her.

"Uncle Obie Watson helped us find the house," Eunice informed him. "Mama drove up his drive by mistake, and he set us straight."

Nick's already stormy face darkened. "Stay away from that man, Violet. He's trouble."

"Whatever do you mean?" she demanded, rounding on him with narrowed eyes.

"Watson's bad through and through. He's got a prison record! I'm telling you, stay away from him!"

It was a poor choice of words. Violet refused to allow two men to dictate to her in one day. She drew herself erect. "Mr. Houghton, you have no right to tell me anything. Good day."

Nick grabbed her arm. "He's after something, Violet. Don't trust him for an instant!"

With an icy glare, Violet ordered, "Unhand me, sir. And stop calling me Violet. I am Mrs. Fairfield to you."

To her surprise, he released her. She picked up her skirts, gathered up her brood, and entered the house, thankful that he did not follow.

❧

Sheriff Boz Martin bent over to study the chestnut gelding's right rear shoe. "Sure enough, Buck, there's a notch on the outside edge. That'll make him easier to track, and the muddy roads will help—but are you sure we can backtrack him more than a mile or two? I think we'd do better to try to trace Fairfield by asking at nearby towns. That way we'd have a general idea which direction he rode."

Obie released Barabbas's leg and straightened, patting the horse's muscular haunch. "It would be quicker to backtrack the horse. He can't have traveled fast or far. Jerry might well be in urgent need of help. I'll go alone if you want to try your way."

Boz twisted his round face into a grimace. "Stubborn cuss. All right, we'll try your way; but I'm warning you, it won't be easy."

The men watered Barabbas and turned him out to pasture before mounting up. The lonely gelding limped along the fence line, following the other horses. When he could go no farther, he craned his thick neck over the top rail and whinnied a plaintive farewell.

Obie followed the trail easily from the saddle, his narrowed eyes picking up each hoofprint in the soft mud. Even

Boz could tell that Barabbas had stopped occasionally to graze by the roadside. "He might not have come far, traveling slowly like this. Else it could be that he's been traveling for a day or two."

"Been little other traffic lately. That helps."

"Fairfield was heading toward Redcliff."

"Likely."

A few hours later they came to a place where Barabbas had emerged onto the main road from the forest. Boz sat back on his saddle, wheezing slightly. His yellowed moustache blew outward with each breath he exhaled. "Now what? Why would Fairfield be traipsin' around in the forest?"

"To keep from meetin' anyone, most likely. There's a passel of Indian trails through these woods. C'mon."

"You're going in there?"

"Of course. A horse crashing through undergrowth makes an easy track to follow." Obie rode Jughead through the ditch and up into the trees. Boz's horse followed unwillingly, ears laid back and eyes rolling.

Branches slapped the men's faces, and insects rose in clouds from beneath the horses' feet. "I was hoping there wouldn't be many bugs, but this heat has brought them out," Obie observed gruffly, slapping at his cheek. Jughead lashed his tail and twitched his skin. Obie squashed a deerfly on the horse's shoulder, leaving a splotch of blood on the white hair. Boz muttered oaths under his breath.

They crashed through a shallow ravine, climbed into a thicket of hardwood saplings, and labored up a ridgeline, following Barabbas's clear track. After more than an hour of arduous trailblazing, Jughead suddenly shied and gave a weird screeching cry. A large dark mound lay ahead, sprawled across the narrow trail. Flies swarmed around it, and an acrid odor filled the air.

Within seconds Obie knelt beside the prostrate body. Boz heaved himself off his horse. "Dead?"

"Not quite. Gut shot." The front of the man's expansive waistcoat was brown, purple, and crimson with dried and fresh blood. The sight of a small hole beside his fourth waist-coat button told the trackers all they needed to know. A bullet in the belly almost inevitably meant a lingering death.

Suddenly his bleary blue eyes opened. "Water," he croaked. Obadiah took his canteen from Jughead's saddle and held it to the injured man's lips. He drank, though most of it dribbled down over his chins. "Thank God," he breathed.

Obie's surprise at the prayer must have shown, for the wounded man's cracked lips twisted into a smile. "Lyin' here, had time. . .make right with God. Buck Watson, forgive me?"

Obie gripped one hot, fleshy hand. "For what?"

"Yuma. Boz, I never killed anyone. Find Fairfield by old chimney. . .road south. Buried him there. . .years ago. Read my letter—tells all. Give all I own to Fairfield's wife, please?"

Obie and Boz exchanged glances. "You're not Jerry Fairfield?"

"Don't know me yet? Charles Bolton. Guess I was. . .a good actor. I knew you right off, Buck, even though you. . . changed your name. It was Patrick done me in. I didn't know him either until he said—" The dying man took a shuddering breath and convulsed, knocking Obie back with one flying arm. "Pain! Oh, God, help me!"

Obie was too stunned by these revelations to speak. Boz tried to question Charles again, but he would only moan, "The letter. Read the letter!"

He soon drifted into an unconscious state, each breath moaning from his lungs.

Still sitting on the ground where he had fallen, Obie stared blankly at the sheriff. "Think he'll come to again?"

"For his sake, I hope not. You still don't recognize him?"

"Twenty years ago he was a skinny kid with curly blond hair and big white teeth."

Boz considered the obese, nearly bald man whose teeth were rotting away and understood Obadiah's lack of perception.

"What letter was he talking about?"

Looking mystified, Boz shrugged. "We'll search him later."

They held solemn vigil over Charles Bolton until the man's

labored breathing stopped entirely. Obie pulled off his shirt and wrapped it around the dead man's face. "I'm thankful he had time to make his soul right with the Lord."

Boz gave him a quizzical look. "If you say so. I wouldn't wish a death like that on a dog. Can you imagine killing your brother that way?"

"Not even my worst enemy. What do we do with him, Boz? Bury him here?"

"What about Mrs. Fairfield?"

Obadiah dropped his head into his hands and rested his elbows on his upraised knees. He ran his fingers through his hair, knocking his hat to the ground. "This is too complicated for me. Charles said he buried the real Jerry Fairfield. . ."

"By the old chimney. I'm thinkin' he meant that burned-out foundation alongside the road to Rockford. You know, the old Miller place?"

Obie was thinking along different lines. "If Patrick shot Charles, he must still be in the area. I wonder if he has been living around here all the time, just like Charles has, and we don't know him. Even Charles didn't know him—his own brother. Patrick was a kid when I last saw him. Twenty years would make quite a difference."

"How old would he be?"

"Thirty-three or -four—and he undoubtedly knows who I am. But if he's been living here for a while, why did he just now kill Jerry—I mean, Charles?"

Boz could only shake his head. "Maybe Charles had the gold?"

"He never mentioned it—but remember how I told you earlier that someone ransacked his house?" Replacing his hat, Obie scrambled to his feet. "C'mon, Boz, we'll grow moss a-sittin' here. Charles needs to be buried quickly, and I think it ought to be in the church graveyard. He may have been a thief and a liar, but God forgave him and so should we."

"Buck, if I was you, I'd want the varmint strung up by the ears."

"He wasn't so bad as all that—just selfish and lazy. Patrick and Edwin were the vicious Boltons, not Charles."

"He let you serve time at Yuma for their crimes. That's vicious enough for me. Wait, let me search him for that letter."

It only took a moment's search. In Charles's left hand, crumpled and filthy, was an envelope with graphite pencil scribbles on both sides. Boz puzzled over it, handed it to Obie, but neither of them could make heads or tails of it. Only a word here and there was legible. "May have to send this away to be analyzed."

"He was dying when he wrote it," Obie defended the departed man. "Can you at least read the signature?"

"Well enough. If he confessed to the robbery, your record should be cleared."

"I had thought of that."

Together the two men loaded Charles Bolton's immense body up on Boz's fidgeting gelding. Although Jughead was the more tractable horse, he was too small to carry such a heavy load. Boz Martin rode the mustang while Obie walked alongside the bay, holding the body in place. This time they followed the trail, and the going was easier.

"What say we don't tell anyone that Charles was alive when we found him?" Boz suggested after a long silence. "And not a word about the letter."

As Obie tramped along, feeling a blister rise on each heel, his mind spun in confused circles. *Lord, help me. The fact that Violet has been a widow for years doesn't excuse me from dreaming about her when I thought she was a married woman. I must be crazy—a man just died a horrible death, Violet's real husband died who knows how or when, and there is a killer loose in the area—yet I feel like shouting for joy because she's free!*

four

"The just man walketh in his integrity:
his children are blessed after him." Proverbs 20:7

Violet awoke to heavy pounding on the boardinghouse's front door. Curious and groggy, she slipped a dress over her chemise. Still buttoning up the front, she stepped out into the hall and listened while Amelia cautiously opened the door. "Obadiah Watson." The lady's voice held little warmth. "What are you doing here? It's too late for social calls, and. . .what has become of your shirt?"

"I need to see Mrs. Fairfield. It's important."

"You cain't barge in and demand to see a lady at this hour—and not even decently dressed! Hev you been drinking?"

"Mrs. Sidwell, the sheriff is here, too. We have information about—"

"Is. . .is that a body hanging over the saddle?" Amelia squealed. "Oh—"

Obie's voice was forceful. "Quiet, ma'am. Don't wake the town. We must speak with Mrs. Fairfield. If you won't fetch her, I'll go up myself."

"That won't be necessary." As though in a trance, Violet descended the stairs, one hand resting on the banister. On the third step she stopped and asked bluntly, "Is my husband alive?"

Looking weary and sorrowful, Obie put one boot on the bottom step. His low voice reached her ears only. "I'm afraid not, ma'am. He's been dead for years."

Violet slowly sank toward the step. "I knew it all the time. And I came all this way—" Suddenly her world went black.

The next thing she knew, Violet vaguely felt herself lifted in strong arms. It was pleasant to rest there against a man's chest. It had been many years since a man had taken care of her. Always she was the caregiver.

Then she gasped and started awake as powerful fumes cleared her head. Amelia sat back, satisfied, and corked her bottle of smelling salts. "Thought that would bring you back to us."

Violet propped herself up on her elbows. She was reclining on the parlor sofa. She and Amelia were alone in the room. "Did you carry me in here?"

"Course not. Obadiah did. He's out talking with the sheriff. I think they're taking the body to the undertaker. I'll go check."

When Amelia was gone, Violet slowly sat up, still feeling lightheaded. She closed her eyes and tried to remember Jeremiah's face, but it had faded from her memory. A tear trickled down her cheek.

"Ma'am?"

Violet looked up into Obie's compassionate eyes. Taking her totally by surprise, a sob tore from her throat. More tears followed. Obie knelt before her and offered a clean handkerchief. Violet blew her nose and wiped her eyes, but the tears would not stop. "I'm sorry!" she gasped. "It's just that. . .oh, everything!"

"I'll listen if you want to talk."

"I. . .I. . .thank you," she sputtered. His calm regard helped her regain control, and soon she poured her troubles upon his sympathetic ear.

". . .and when I received the package containing his watch, purse, and other personal effects, I knew he was dead. I had already suspected as much, for he had not written to me, and Jeremiah was a faithful correspondent. There was no letter in the package, nothing to tell me how or where he died. I didn't know what to do. I was living with my in-laws in Maryland at the time, and neither of them was well—they have since passed on. I simply mourned my husband for a year, then moved on with my life."

"Did you not have friends at church who would help you? What about your family?"

She studied the wadded handkerchief and confessed, "My parents were far away in Connecticut, and I was too proud or too shy to ask for outside advice. Our pastor never pressed me for details about Jeremiah's death; he simply accepted my word about it. Then, only a few weeks ago, I received an anonymous telegram from Longtree informing me that Jeremiah Fairfield was living here. It shocked and terrified me, you can imagine, to think that my husband might yet be living, for it implied that he had deserted me. This was beyond my imagining; Jeremiah always doted on me and adored his children. Also, he was a good and godly man. I knew that he would never voluntarily abandon us."

Obie nodded. "Of course not."

"Can you explain this mystery? I've been living under a dreadful cloud of apprehension ever since that telegram arrived. How do you know for certain that Jeremiah is. . . dead?"

Obie eased himself up to sit on the sofa beside her, and Violet sat back to listen. "Mr. Fairfield apparently died more than four years ago. While traveling here, he met a man named Charles Bolton. Since Bolton told us that he didn't kill anyone, I assume your husband died of natural causes. Bolton buried him and took his name and identity. The disguise worked for several years, but someone must've suspected him—and whoever it was sent that telegram to you. When your reply arrived, Bolton panicked, ran, and was shot. Before he died, he confessed his true identity and told us where your husband is buried. We will hunt for the grave as soon as possible."

Violet blinked. Oddly enough, she noticed right then that only the top of Obie's red combinations covered his upper body. His suspender straps dangled around his waist. He did still have a blue neckerchief knotted around his tanned throat, but his hairy chest showed beneath it. At another time she might have been tempted to laugh.

She returned her gaze to his sober eyes. "There is more to this story, I'm sure. What do you need me to do?"

"We need you to come to the sheriff's office. He'll tell us both what to do."

"It's late to call for a buggy."

"I'll put you on Jughead. It's only a short way."

Violet regarded her delicate muslin gown. "But—" This was no time to worry about getting her dress dirty. "All right. I need to ask Amelia to keep an eye on the children."

Minutes later she was perched sideways on Jughead's saddle, her legs dangling over the horse's left shoulder. It was not a comfortable seat and she could feel the rhythm of each hoofbeat. Sometimes her feet bumped against Obie, who walked beside his horse.

The town was dark and still, yet Violet felt safe with Obie. She looked up at the stars and sighed. *Back to being a widow—not that I ever stopped feeling like one. How will I tell the children about this? Maybe I should never have told them about the telegram.*

Jughead stopped before the sheriff's office. A light glowed in the window. Obie lifted Violet down. "Go on inside. I'll be a minute," he ordered, fiddling with Jughead's cinch and reins.

Inside the office, by the dim light of a lamp, Violet saw the sheriff draped across his chair, snoring deeply. She cleared her throat, but he never flinched. "Sheriff?" she said, then louder, "Sheriff Martin?"

One final snort and his boots hit the floorboards. "Huh? What?" He grabbed the gun on his hip. "Oh, ma'am, you're here." He rubbed his fleshy face with one hand, looking sleepy and sheepish. "Where's Buck?"

"Buck?"

"Watson. Buck Watson. I can't call him Obie. It just don't fit him."

"He'll be right in. Since it's very late, can we get to the point? Mr. Watson tells me that the man you all thought was Jeremiah was actually someone else, and now this someone else is dead."

"Bolton gave us the location of your husband's grave. We'll verify his statements as soon as possible." The sheriff looked bored. "Ma'am, I'll be brief. Bolton's murderer could be just about anyone in this town. For now, we need to keep quiet all the facts around Bolton's death, all right?"

Violet nodded, wide-eyed. "But people won't understand how I know that I am a widow."

The sheriff pursed his lips, glancing up as Obie entered. "We could just let people think that you refused to view the body, so you wouldn't know about the impersonation. That's reasonable, and it's happened before when a body is battered or decomposed. That way the murderer will think we don't know about Charles and the gold."

Violet shuddered and looked pale. Obie quickly drew up a chair for her and she sat down. "Gold?" she inquired weakly.

"That's a story for another day. It explains why Bolton was killed, but it doesn't involve you, ma'am, so don't worry about it. By the way, one of the last things Charles said was that you were to have his house and all he owned. I think he wanted to make it up to you—make up for using your husband's name, I mean."

"The house. . .is mine?" Violet breathed in awe. "But. . .it was never Jeremiah's. How. . . ? Isn't there someone related to this man who would rightfully inherit his property?"

Obie and Boz exchanged looks. "Charles's brother shot him. If he steps forward and claims the farm, we'll nail him for murder. I don't think he'll be that stupid," Boz said. "Their father died in an Apache raid years ago, and their mother died in childbirth. The eldest brother was killed twenty years ago. There are no other relatives that we know of."

Obie's face looked grim. "The gold originally belonged to another man in New Mexico Territory, but he died in the same Apache raid."

"How horrible!"

"That entire settlement was wiped out, though I've heard that more Americans have moved in since. It's a dangerous area and likely always will be until the Apaches are subdued once and for all."

"That'll be the day," Boz scoffed.

Obie only lifted his brows. "Boz, if you're done, I'll take Mrs. Fairfield back to Amelia's. She looks exhausted."

"She's not the only one. We'll plan the funeral, ma'am. Charles will have to be buried under your husband's name until the mystery is solved. Hope you don't mind."

Rising, Violet took Obie's offered arm. "I don't mind. May I tell the children the true story?"

"I'd rather you didn't. I'm not asking you to lie; just tell them that we need to keep them in the dark for a while. They'll find out everything in the end. Good night, Mrs. Fairfield. I'm sorry ya have to be involved in all this."

"Good night, Sheriff, and thank you for all you're doing."

Obie tightened Jughead's girth again before lifting Violet to the saddle. Strange, how she enjoyed his touch while Nick Houghton's left her feeling soiled.

It was a beautiful night, starry and cool—a perfect night for romance, not for murder and mystery. It wasn't difficult to imagine slipping down from the saddle into Obadiah Watson's strong arms. She had never kissed a man with a moustache before, and she suddenly wanted to try it. Obie's moustache covered most of his upper lip. It would probably tickle, but it wouldn't get in the way of a kiss.

Buck Watson. He had once been called "Buck." She could easily imagine him as a young, lithe, virile cowboy with a gun on his hip and a wicked sparkle in his eyes. Even now, in spite of his gentle ways and silvery hair, he impressed her as a man of action and restrained passion. He made her feel womanly and desirable. She hadn't felt that way in many long years, and she liked it exceedingly.

Shocked by her own thoughts, she sat up straighter and closed her eyes. *I shouldn't be dreaming of romance at a time like this, yet. . . Lord, even though I loved Jeremiah, I have learned, during the last five years, to live without him. I can't even say that I miss him anymore, though memories of our past together will always be sweet. Am I wrong to wish to go on with life and perhaps find a new love?*

Her eyes lowered to Obie's flat hat and square shoulders.

All romance aside, this man is hardworking, kind, and, from what I've seen, he's committed fully to You. My children like him very much, and. . .so do I.

ஐ

"I hate to disturb you two, but the children will be downstairs in a minute or two." Amelia's voice disturbed Violet's slumber. Wincing, she tried to stretch her legs, but they were folded into a cramped position. She reached a hand up and felt the arm of the sofa. Her eyes flew open. She was lying on the parlor sofa, fully clothed but for her hat and shoes. Her hastily pinned-up braid had come loose during the night and wrapped across her face like a soft, thick, frazzled rope.

She sat up and blinked. Across the room, Obie slumped in one of Amelia's stiff chairs, arms dangling over the chair arms, booted feet extended on the hooked rug. He was fast asleep. A patch of hairy chest showed through where a button was missing from his red combinations. His jaw was dark with whiskers. To Violet he looked. . .huggable.

"Obadiah, wake up!" she called gently. "Why are we sleeping in Amelia's parlor? I don't even remember arriving."

Obie reached up to rub his forehead and yawned, starting to stretch. He groaned, reaching for the small of his back—and froze when he spotted Violet. "Mrs. Fairfield!" His voice was gruff. Violet had never before noticed the thick black lashes framing his eyes, for the piercing gray eyes themselves usually commanded her full attention.

"Mama?" It was Samuel, standing in the doorway. "What happened? Why are you down here already?"

"Oh, my dear," Violet sighed, recalling the news she had yet to tell the children. "Where are your sisters?"

"Getting dressed. Hello, Uncle Obie. Did you sleep here all night?"

"Good morning, Samuel. Yes, most of the night."

"Uncle?" Violet questioned.

"That's what all the kids call him. He said I could."

Obie turned to Violet. "With your permission, of course."

"I don't mind if you don't." She lifted a hand to smooth

her hair and saw his eyes follow the motion. She had no memory of arriving home. Had he carried her inside and removed her shoes and hat? "Did I. . .did I fall asleep on your horse?"

"Yes, ma'am. Almost fell off backwards."

Her eyes widened. He must have caught her. Blood heated her face.

"You were terribly tired, ma'am. No shame in that." His voice was tender, soothing. "Want me to stay a while? I will, if you need me."

Violet wasn't sure which of her turbulent emotions caused the lump in her throat. She nodded. "I will bring the girls down and we can all discuss this together."

When Violet returned with her daughters, Samuel was nestled against Obie's side on the davenport, avidly listening. ". . .and that squirrel fooled Treat so completely, she looked silly for days afterward, hunting around that stump as though she expected to find him there. And all the time he was laughing at her from his back doorway."

Samuel chuckled; then he frowned at his mother and sisters. "You came too soon."

"Mama says it's important," Beulah informed him. She and Eunice looked apprehensive. They perched quietly on Amelia's fancy carved chairs, studying their mother's pale face.

Violet stood on the hearth, preparing to speak, but her knees felt rubbery. Moving to the davenport, she sat beside Samuel, drawing strength from Obie's presence. Samuel shifted to lean against her, and she hugged his small body.

"Last night I learned that your father is truly dead after all. He died and was buried more than four years ago, not long after he left us." Violet's voice broke. She squeezed her eyes shut, trying to hold back the tears. Seeking comfort, she reached out to Obadiah. He took her hand and pressed her fingers to assure her of his support.

The girls stared at the floor. Beulah sighed. "I always knew it. Father would never have deserted us. During our train trip out here, I kept thinking about the way he kissed you good-bye that last time, as though he would never let go."

"I wonder if he knew he wouldn't come back?" Eunice pondered quietly.

Violet continued, "We may keep the house. Your father would have wanted us to enjoy living in it, I'm sure."

She interrupted questioning exclamations to explain, "The man who has been using your father's name was killed yesterday. We must pretend for a while that he was really your father. I can't explain it all to you right now, but the sheriff has asked us to do this to help him catch the murderer. Do you understand?"

"Not really, Mama, but I'll try to pretend."

"Do you mean we need to cry at a funeral and stuff like that?"

"Must we go into mourning again?" Eunice groaned.

Violet sympathized. "It won't be fun, but I'm sure we can do it. Just think about your father, and don't talk to *anyone* about what happened, all right?"

"Except for Uncle Obie. He's our friend." Samuel pulled away from Violet and moved closer to Obadiah, who wrapped his arm around the father-hungry boy and hugged him close.

Violet watched them and felt a stirring of joy. "Obie, would you pray for us?" she asked suddenly.

"Yes. I've been thinking of a Bible verse that describes your family," he stated. "It's found in Proverbs: 'The just man walketh in his integrity: his children are blessed after him.' Children, from what I've heard about your father, this verse describes him well."

Holding hands, they all knelt on the floor before the sofa, and Obie prayed aloud, requesting God's healing touch upon the Fairfield family, His guidance for their future, and His blessing on all their ways. After the "Amen," Violet watched as each of her children gave Obie a fond and grateful hug—even Beulah.

"I must get home, Mrs. Fairfield. Al and Myles will be wondering about me." Obie picked his hat off a side table and brushed imaginary dirt from its brim. "I'll check on you soon."

five

"Here it is, Boz. Charles carved Fairfield's initials on the cross-beam." Obie lifted his lantern to examine the crude wooden cross that stood in the lee of a crumbling rock chimney.

Boz approached, threw down his cigarette, and removed his hat in respect for the dead. "Not much question now that she's a widow," he observed.

Obie gave him a sharp look. "You having thoughts about marriage, Boz?"

The sheriff's moustache puffed outward. "Mebbe some thoughts, but no expectations. She's a fine woman—too fine for the likes of us. This Jeremiah Fairfield musta been quite a man to catch a woman like her."

Obadiah said nothing, but his moustache twitched as he contemplated his friend's words.

"You're sweet on her, ain't you?" Boz observed.

Obie nodded silently.

"Thinking she's the little woman God sent your way?"

"Maybe."

Boz's wheezing laughter disturbed the quiet grave site. "I cain't believe you, Buck! Still believe that God answers your prayers? You've lost what little sense you ever had."

"God can work miracles, Boz. I know, somehow, that He's going to clear my name. Surely, you can't help but see how everything is coming together. Bolton's confession, the letter—he maybe even told on that envelope where the gold is hidden. Can't you see? God promised that His justice will prevail—and even if I don't live to see it, I know that the truth will win out eventually."

"Buck, ol' boy, let me make you a deal. If your name is cleared of this crime and you marry Violet Fairfield, I promise I'll believe that there is a God."

Obie's head snapped around. "No fooling? You'd better think hard before you strike a bargain with God. If you decide that He exists, the next logical step is to give your life to Him."

Boz lifted his right hand. "I swear it. I'm not worried; there's no chance that I'll lose. I think the world of you, Buck, but let's face it: You're no prize. What have you got to offer a woman like Violet Fairfield? Pigs'll fly from pine trees before she marries the likes of you."

"You may be right, Boz. But I do know that God has a sense of humor, and you just challenged Him to prove you wrong. I've got more hope of Violet marryin' me now than I ever did before!" Obadiah's eyes glimmered in the lamplight.

❧

It was four days after the funeral. The children were busy with school and activities with their new friends. Violet found time weighing heavy on her hands. She was unaccustomed to idleness.

"Amelia?"

"In the scullery, ma'am. You needin' anything?" Amelia Sidwell backed out of her storage closet with a sack of cornmeal in her hands.

"I wanted to ask if you need anything at the store today. I plan to walk over to the parsonage this morning. Mrs. Schoengard keeps asking me to drop by, and I have plenty of time now."

Amelia understood the unspoken "now that the funeral is over."

"Any word on when you can move out to the house? I understand there were some legal questions to settle first, but it does seem that a woman should have clear claim to her husband's property. I hate to be takin' your money when you could be settlin' into your own place."

"I might stop by the sheriff's office and ask about that. So, do you need anything?"

"Not that I can think of at the moment. You just go on and have yourself a good time. Iffen the children come home before you're back, I'll keep watch over 'em. Don't you worry yourself none."

"Yes, ma'am."

Violet didn't bother to request a buggy. The center of town was only a few streets from Amelia's boardinghouse, and the parsonage was even closer. She wore sturdy walking shoes, a black gown, and a black straw bonnet. It was depressing to be back in mourning, but she understood the necessity. . .for the time being.

Without realizing it, she kept her eyes peeled for a glimpse of Obadiah Watson. She hadn't seen him since the funeral. He had acted as a pallbearer for his erstwhile neighbor—in spite of protests from a few townspeople who considered him a suspect in the murder. Violet had heard murmurs from various sources that caused her to wonder what scandal lay in his past. "Buck" Watson might have been wilder than she had imagined.

Caroline Schoengard welcomed her warmly. "Violet, dear, please come in! You caught me in the midst of baking pies. My mother-in-law is watching the children for me so I can get some work done."

Violet chuckled. "I know how that goes. Put me to work, Caroline. It's always easier to talk with busy hands."

So Caroline assigned her the task of picking through and hulling strawberries. Violet laid aside her bonnet and gloves, donned a spare apron, and set to work. "It's nice to feel useful again," she confided. "I do love Amelia, but she doesn't want another woman in her kitchen. Anything I do, she does over again her way. It's enough to make me feel like a second-rate homemaker!"

Caroline smiled as she rolled out pastry. "She is an exacting person, but no one can fault her as a friend. She'll stick with you through anything, Violet, and I happen to know that she thinks highly of you and of your children. She's been concerned about you since your husband's sudden death. It must have been an awful shock, coming all the way out here only to have him murdered on the day after your arrival."

Violet felt awkward. She didn't want to lie to her friend, yet it seemed rude to say nothing. "It would have been worse, perhaps, if it hadn't been so long since we last saw him. I had a premonition that things would never be the same for us. Perhaps the Lord was preparing me for the. . .the strange occurrences to come."

With a sideward glance, Caroline considerately dropped the subject. "What do you think of our town? People are speculating about whether or not you'll stay in Longtree now that Jerry's gone. You could sell the Folly—I hope you don't mind that name for your place?"

"Not at all."

"Good. Anyway, you could sell the house for a good price, I'm sure. It's rather fancy for the location; but the farmland is premium, and it's close to town."

Violet rinsed and sliced several berries and dropped them into the bowl before replying, "I have no plans to sell at present. The children are happy here. They have made many new friends, and all three wish to keep the Folly. It is far finer than any house we've lived in before—including my parents' home in Connecticut. This is a pleasant town, and the scenery around here is wonderful—so many trees and lakes. We have no desire to live anywhere else."

"The winters are harsh, let me warn you."

"I'm sure we will adjust. I prefer cold weather to hot, humid weather. I tend to wilt in the heat." After a long pause she continued, "Caroline, I did have a particular reason for coming to see you today."

Caroline pricked the pie shells with a fork. "I thought you might."

Violet sat back in her chair, resting her hands on the berry bucket. "In Annapolis we had a visitation ministry in which certain members of the church volunteered their time to help out those in need, such as widows, the elderly and infirm, or those with sick family members. We would clean, cook, bake, make repairs, or simply read aloud—whatever the person needed most. Is there any such ministry at this church right now?"

Caroline tried to conceal a smile. "Nothing is organized, but you're not the first person to express interest in this type of ministry."

"That's wonderful! Do you think there are enough of us to form a 'care committee,' or is that not an option?" Violet's hands flew as her excitement grew.

"I'll discuss it with David tonight. Don't you really know who does most of this type of work in our community?"

Violet looked closely at her new friend. "Should I know?"

Caroline grinned. "Do you have enough berries ready to fill these two shells? I'd like to get the first two pies in the oven while we fix the rest."

Violet helped fill the shells and add the top crusts, but her mind was full of questions. Once the pies were in the oven, she cornered Caroline. "Why do I feel as though I'm missing something important here?"

Caroline shook her head. "I'm sorry, honey. It's just that I can't help wondering if God has a secret plan. Your sudden arrival, the strange happenings, the feeling of mystery in town. . ."

"Caroline, you're not answering my question. Why did you look amused when I asked about a visitation ministry?"

Caroline rolled her blue eyes and brushed back a wisp of blond hair. "Because Obadiah Watson is practically David's assistant pastor in this community. He voluntarily takes food to the elderly, sits with the sick, works around other people's farms when they are laid up—nearly everything that you just professed interest in doing. Now do you understand why I smiled? I don't mean to be nosy, but I couldn't help thinking how ideal it would be if you and he made a match. I know you're only recently widowed and probably need time before you'll feel ready for remarriage, but, well. . . Do you see what I mean?"

Violet felt the tide of blood roll into her face, but she was helpless to stop it. "Oh."

"Now I've gone and made you uncomfortable." Caroline wiped her hands on her apron and placed an arm around Violet's shoulders. She was a tall woman with a sturdy frame and Violet felt like a child beside her, although she was several years older than the pastor's wife.

"I don't mean to interfere, Violet. I hope you know that David and I only want the best for you and your family. I'm so thankful you're here in town. I've needed a friend—someone I could talk to about the Lord and about personal matters. I've seen a tender spirit in you, and I know that your walk with the Lord is genuine and sincere. You're not a gossip, and you're a fine mother. No matter what rumors circulate about you, I can judge for myself that you're the kind of person this town needs."

Violet's heart warmed. Caroline might be lacking in tact, but she was unaffected and truly kind. "Thank you, Caroline," she murmured. "I need you, too."

⋅᪶⋅

After partaking of a generous luncheon of ham sandwiches, baked beans, and strawberry pie, Violet took leave of the parsonage. In marked contrast to her sober attire, there was a spring in her step and a light in her eyes as she headed toward town. Caroline's offer of true friendship had been exactly what she needed. It was good to know that someone, another woman, believed in her no matter how odd the circumstances of her arrival had seemed.

Sheriff Martin sat in front of his office, cleaning a rifle. At Violet's approach, he set down his front chair legs and invited her inside. "I been meanin' to ride over for a talk with you, ma'am."

"I was simply wondering what progress had been made on your. . .investigation." Violet followed him into the stuffy, smelly office. Through an open door behind his desk, she saw a row of jail cells. Someone back there warbled an off-key ditty that made conversation somewhat difficult.

The sheriff yelled for the singer to "knock off" and closed the door with a bang. "Sorry, ma'am. He's supposed to be sleepin' it off; he went on a real spree last night."

"I see." Violet accepted an offered chair, though its seat was torn and springs extruded from the holes. She sat gingerly, wishing she had not come. The other night, when Obie had accompanied her, she had not noticed the condition of the office. Neither had she noticed the unsavory habits of the sheriff. He shifted a chaw into his other cheek and spat toward the corner. A glob streaked down the wall near the cuspidor, joining others of its kind.

The smells in this building nearly overpowered Violet. She unobtrusively pulled a scented handkerchief, edged in black lace, from her reticule and lifted it to her nose.

Martin settled into his creaking chair. "Mrs. Fairfield, I'm sorry to mention such a. . .an unpleasant thing, but Buck 'n' me found your real husband's grave the other night."

Violet felt thankful to be sitting down.

"There was a wooden cross marking the spot, with J.F. carved on the crossbeam. There's no doubt that it's Jeremiah Fairfield's grave. We left the body undisturbed for now."

She nodded. "Where's Mr. Watson?"

Boz gave her a close look. "At his farm, I reckon, or with Hattie Thwaite. He spends a lot of time with her. Why?"

Obie had a lady friend? Why had she not been told? "I just wondered," she said lamely, feeling small and alone. "I do appreciate all the trouble you've gone to for me."

"It's part of my job. Can't say I enjoy it, but it had to be done." Violet could hear him breathing. A heavy man with a barrel chest, he wheezed like a blacksmith's bellows. "I'm sorry you can't give your husband a Christian burial right now. He can be reburied at the church once this mystery is solved."

Violet nodded. "I'm sure he doesn't care. He's too busy enjoying heaven to worry about a headstone over his body here on earth."

Boz looked surprised and impressed. "That's one way to look at it. You're sure he's in heaven, huh?"

"Yes. Jeremiah knew the Lord well."

"Like Buck does." Without looking for a reply, the sheriff said, "You can move out to the house anytime you like. Strange that it's called Fairfield's Folly when 'twasn't a Fairfield what built it. Kinda prophetic in a way. Reckon you'll want to clean. I checked it out after Buck told me about the break-in. It's a mess."

"I will send for my furniture right away," Violet brightened. "We'll have plenty of time to clean before our things arrive. You're sure it's rightfully ours?"

"Sure as I can be. No one else claims it, and Charles himself willed it to you. Buck and me are witnesses to that, and we wrote down his last words in case your claim is ever contested. I had a lawyer check things out, and he's handling all the legal work. He'll have some papers for you to sign, no doubt, but for now you're free to move in. If you need any help, let me know." Sheriff Martin smiled, or at least his face crinkled up and his tobacco-stained moustache lifted at the corners.

"Thank you, Sheriff." Since the interview seemed at an end, she rose with a rustle of petticoats and extended her black-gloved hand. "I appreciate all you have done for us."

"I ain't done much. The Schoengards did the funeral, and Buck arranged for the coffin and the hearse and all. By the way, you did a fine imitation of a grieving widow at that service, ma'am, and I'm appreciatin' how you've gone into mourning like your husband really just passed on. You've helped us more than we've helped you."

"I don't think that is possible. By the way, Sheriff, may I ask why you call Mr. Watson 'Buck'?"

"That was his name back when I met him. He started going by Obadiah a while back, but he'll always be Buck to me."

"How long have you known him?" Violet forgot about leaving.

"Oh, we were wild young cowhands together out West many years back. Then our ways parted, and I heard about his conviction. Always figgered it was a frame job. I met up with Buck after his release. He says he 'met God' while he was in prison. Seems a strange place to meet the Almighty, but I cain't deny the change in Buck Watson. He was lucky to live through Yuma—not many could survive it."

Prison? "What was he like before?" Violet asked, trying not to sound shocked.

The sheriff gave her a penetrating look. His moustache twitched from side to side as he chewed solemnly, rather like a cow. "Back in the fifties we worked as hired guns, cowpunchers, horse breakers, or as trail guides for wagon trains. Anything to make a living. Buck always had honor, though, and he never placed value on gettin' rich. If he says he didn't rob the DeVries gold shipment, I believe him."

Violet's eyes were large. She swallowed hard. This was more information than she was prepared to assimilate at the moment.

"I may regret this, but I'll tell you somethin' else, ma'am. Buck's always been honorable where women are concerned. He'd make a fine husband, if you're thinkin' on those lines."

Violet plucked at her cuffs with nervous fingers and tucked her reticule under one arm. "I like and admire Mr. Watson, sir, but marriage is far from my mind at this time." She hoped the second part was not a total lie. She wanted to ask about Hattie Thwaite, but did not have the courage. Prison sentence? So Houghton had not lied about Obie after all.

The afternoon was waning into evening shadows when Violet stepped out upon the boardwalk. Not many people were on the street at this hour. Sighing, Violet started back toward Amelia's. Another day without a glimpse of Obadiah Watson. Was he working at his farm or helping a needy family. . .or entertaining another woman?

"Violet!" a masculine voice hailed from across the street. Violet tried not to grimace. She did her best to avoid Nick Houghton, but he had a way of popping up anywhere and everywhere. The man was impossible to discourage, it seemed. He hurried across the street, holding his hat in place. The sunset lighted his bright eyes and dazzling smile. A mane of golden brown hair flowed to his shoulders, and thick side-whiskers emphasized his square chin.

"Hello, Mr. Houghton. How are you this evening?" Violet did not offer her hand.

"Fine, now that I've seen you. Violet, I've seen few women who look ravishing in mourning, but you top my list of lovely widows. What were you doing in the sheriff's office?"

"He had a few questions to clear up. He's investigating my husband's death, you see. Now I must be going, sir, as I have not yet supped this evening."

"Hurrah! I've been longing to take you to dinner, my dear. This is my lucky night."

"I don't believe that would be proper, Mr. Houghton. I am in mourning, you know."

"Fiddlesticks! As though anyone in Longtree cares about such niceties. What could be more public and innocent than supper in the hotel dining room?"

"I thank you, but no. Amelia will have saved supper for me, and I must be getting on home." Violet increased her pace, but Nick's long legs had no trouble matching it.

"How are you, Violet? I haven't really had a chance to ask since the funeral. Such a shocking thing, Jerry's death! A robbery, I suppose they've decided."

"I am as well as can be expected," she answered honestly. "The children keep me occupied. They are making many friends here. Although school will be out for the summer in a few weeks, I have encouraged them to attend. It has helped them adjust to our altered circumstances."

"So you intend to stay here? Why don't you sell out and move back East?"

"I like it here." For the first time she questioned her own motives. Why did she like it here so much? It was a beautiful setting, but scenery was not the reason for her determination to stay.

Nick blurted, "Violet, my dear, you must be reasonable. This is no place for a lady like you."

"I am being reasonable. The people here are kind and helpful, and I love the trees and the lakes—"

"You won't be so enthusiastic come January. This place is an icebox for months on end, and there is little to do for entertainment. I can't bear to think of you alone in that house—"

"Hardly alone with three children."

"—alone in the wilderness. Helpless. You cannot begin to conceive of the difficulties you would encounter. You could never manage that farm alone. You must marry if you plan to stay."

Marry! Violet stopped in her tracks and stared at him. She noted the slight puffiness under his eyes, the broken blood vessels in his nose, and the red wetness of his lips beneath a heavy moustache.

"Mr. Houghton—"

"Nicholas."

"—Nicholas, I feel more at home here in Longtree than I ever did in Annapolis. I don't mind the cold, and I don't mind the lack of big-city entertainment. If I marry again, it will be for love, not out of necessity. The children and I have managed to survive for several years while my husband was away, and we will manage equally well here. We are not afraid of hard work."

"My dear lady, you may need protection. Your husband was murdered, after all. Who's to say the killer would not harm you? I don't mean to alarm you, but I am concerned for your safety, Violet. I would protect and shield you from harm if you would allow me to."

Violet crossed the street and resumed her rapid pace. "I appreciate your offer, but I don't believe I'm in any danger."

Houghton grabbed her arm and pinned her with his blue stare. "I think you ought to know that a convicted murderer lives on the farm next to the Folly. It's only a matter of time before he's brought in for questioning about Jerry's death. Violet, listen to me—you must not move out there without a man for protection! Anything could happen."

"What are you talking about? Convicted murderer?" Violet hoped her confusion looked genuine.

"Everyone knows that Buck Watson killed several men and

robbed a private gold shipment twenty years ago in New Mexico. He was a legendary gunman, but somehow he managed to slip the noose."

Violet recalled Boz's certainty of Obie's innocence, but she still felt slightly ill. "I cannot believe it. Obadiah Watson is no murderer. He can't be!" She remembered the bashful way he lifted her down from his horse, the grip of his strong hand when she reached out for his support, his loving hugs for the children, his deep voice lifted in prayer. . . Yet he *had* served a prison sentence. Could this horrible accusation be true?

She pulled her arm out of Houghton's grasp and hurried along the dirt walkway that led to Amelia's boardinghouse.

"You seem eager to defend the fellow. What's he to you?"

Violet tried to speak boldly, but her voice trembled. "A friend and brother in the Lord."

Houghton's jaw worked as though he gritted his teeth, but almost immediately his smile reappeared. "Research the crime for yourself then. The facts in the case will be hard to ignore. The man is a killer beyond all doubt. The jury found him guilty. His death sentence was hung up on a mere triviality."

"How do you know so much about it?"

For an instant he looked startled. "When a man with a shady past moves into a community, concerned citizens make sure they know what they're up against. I'm not the only one who has investigated the case."

"Doesn't the sheriff know about it?"

"That dolt! He's the poorest excuse for a sheriff I've ever encountered. All he ever does is clean his guns and lounge around his office. He sends his deputy out to do all the legwork. Someday he'll break his fat neck when his easy chair slips, and the town will hold a celebration."

Violet was grateful to see the picket fence around Amelia's yard not far ahead. Soon she could escape from this annoying man. "If the sheriff is that incompetent, I wonder why he keeps being reappointed."

"This is off the subject, Violet. No matter what you choose to believe about Watson, your life could be in grave danger."

"I'll take my chances. I don't believe he would harm me."

"If you had seen him pick a man off a running horse with one rifle shot while lying flat on his back, maybe you wouldn't be so pert. He's deadly."

"Have you seen Obadiah Watson do that? I don't believe it." Violet tried to keep her voice calm. "He doesn't even carry a gun."

At Amelia's gate, Nick grabbed Violet again and spun her about. "The point here is that I want you to trust me! It hurts that you don't trust my assessment of the situation. I want to be part of your life and your decisions."

He raised a hand to forestall her protest. "I realize that we met only a few days ago and that you are but newly widowed, but I knew the moment I laid eyes on you that our destinies were to be intertwined. Long hours have I listened to Jerry praise your beauty and warmth; little did I know that one day I would be able to appreciate your assets for myself." His eyes lowered to her body in a way Violet found insulting.

She flung off his hands. "Mr. Houghton, I have reason neither to trust you nor to believe a word that you say. I know nothing good of you, and you manage to insult me in some way at our every meeting. Now I must bid you good evening."

ප

Nick watched her rush up the path. This Fairfield woman was proving more difficult than he had anticipated. She seemed to have developed an aversion to his company, and Nick was unaccustomed to having women find him distasteful. The novelty did not improve his temper. "I'll have her yet," he determined. "She is one handsome woman worth having."

six

*" 'Behold the fowls of the air: for they sow not, neither do
they reap, nor gather into barns; yet your heavenly
Father feedeth them. Are ye not much better than they?' "*
Matthew 6:26

Al watched his cousin scrape whiskers and soap from his face
with the long razor. "I don't blame you, Cousin Buck. She's a
handsome woman—and for that matter, her daughters are no
hardship to the eyes. I wouldn't mind paying a call on Beulah.
Never did see prettier eyes on a girl."

"I have. Her mother's eyes." Obie splashed water on his
smooth face and toweled off. "Thought I liked brown eyes best
until I saw Violet's blue ones." He combed back his damp hair,
peering into the bleary mirror.

"She can't be much younger than you, since Beulah is at
least sixteen. Course, maybe she married young. She doesn't
look very old—the mother, I mean. I saw the way you two hit
it off that first day when she was here. No, don't say it—I
know you weren't trying to flirt with a married woman, but the
understanding, the. . .the. . .what's the word I'm looking for?"

"Esteem? Affinity?" Obie hauled on a chambray shirt, but-
toned it, and snapped his suspenders in place. Digging a clean
neckerchief from his bureau drawer, he tied it haphazardly
about his neck.

"Affinity, that's it. The affinity between you two was obvious even to me. And now she's a widow! Maybe God sent
her here so you two could meet and fall in love." Al tagged
along behind his cousin as Obie clapped his hat on and
headed toward the barn.

"Al—"

"There's nothing wrong with that. I know you wouldn't

72

have tried to steal her from Fairfield if he had lived."

Obie stopped in his tracks, propped fists on his hips, and glared up at the tall boy. "I envied him, Al, and I coveted her. I can't deny it."

"But you repented, put your desires aside, and acted honorably. God will forgive your human failings, Cousin Buck."

Staring at the ground, Obie considered the boy's words. "How'd you get to be so smart, kid?"

"Walk with the wise, and you will be wise," Al responded with a grin. "I haven't lived with you all these years for nothing!"

Inside the barn, Al hopped up and sat upon Brunhilda's stall door. A chorus of piggy squeals rose from behind him. "You're taking Barabbas to her? I doubt she'll care for him. Maybe you'd better help her find a milder horse."

"I'll let her make that decision; she has a good mind of her own. I hear she's talking about buying a horse, but she already owns this one." Obie's dark brows drew together in concern. "Look, I've got to be careful, Al. As soon as I start thinking maybe I could have a chance with her, my common sense rears its head and I know better. When I start putting my wants ahead of God's perfect plan, I'm in trouble."

"How do you know that your wants aren't in God's plan?"

Obie clenched his fists and slammed one into the seat of a saddle on its rack. "I don't know. But I've got to be careful. I want to help her, Al. All the time I want to be with her. . .but I'm afraid. That's the honest truth. I'm afraid of what she'll say when she hears about my criminal record. Maybe she's already heard and she'll cut me dead today. I don't know. I'm afraid she'd laugh in my face if I ever told her how I feel about her."

"From what I saw, I don't think so. She seems to respect and admire you, Cousin. I think you might have a chance with her. It's about time you settled down and had a family."

Obie snorted and shook his head. His former hope now seemed like striving after the wind.

Al wasn't finished. "I think God sent her in answer to

prayer: One woman, made to order."

"What makes you think I've been praying for a wife?" Obie growled, hauling Jughead's saddle from the rack.

"Maybe you haven't, but I've been praying on your behalf. If any man ever deserved a good woman, it's you. Ma always said. . ."

Obie hurried outside. Al's voice faded away.

≥°

Violet entered Amelia's kitchen. "Amelia, do you know where I could find some gentle horses like yours? I've put off purchasing horses and a rig because I haven't the first idea how to go about it. I suppose I could pay to have my dry goods and groceries delivered to the house, but we still have to own some means of transportation. Nick Houghton is right about that, at any rate."

"Won't he help you find a horse?" Amelia stopped peeling potatoes to examine her boarder's face.

"I'm sure he would if I were to ask, but I do not desire his help."

Amelia's long fingers wielded a knife with such speed that the peeling seemed to fall from a potato of its own volition. "Nick's not used to a woman running the other way; most of 'em swarm him like flies."

"Indeed?" Violet picked up a knife and started peeling.

"Ya don't need to do that, honey."

"I know, but I might as well work while I chat. We've been in Longtree for nearly a month now, and I want so much to move into our house, yet it could be weeks before our furniture arrives. Do you think I would be crazy to move out there with no beds, just blankets to sleep on?"

"It's been done before. Do whatever you like, honey. You're in charge of your own life, you know."

Just then Beulah called, "Mama, Mr. Watson is out front and he wants to see you."

"Oh!" Violet hopped up, dropped her half-peeled potato back into the bowl, and smoothed her dress.

Amelia stopped to watch her with an amused smirk. "Miz

Fairfield, and your first man hardly cold in his grave! You'll set tongues to waggin', though not many would blame you. A woman with younguns needs a man about the house. Obie ain't so grand to look at, but he'll provide well for ya. Used to figger on snatchin' him up for myself, but he's too partic'lar to settle for a skinny ol' biddy like me."

She picked up the abandoned potato and finished peeling it. "You may not be too handy about the house, but he'll likely be happy jest to sit and stare at yer pretty face. Some men got that romantic streak, and nothing seems to cure 'em of it."

Violet fled the kitchen, feeling much warmer than the weather justified. She peeked through the front window. Sure enough, Obie waited at the gate. The sight of his trim figure made her chest feel constricted, as though her corset were laced too tightly. Since the funeral she had seen him only at church, where they had simply exchanged polite pleasantries. Maybe he was aware of her interest and, in his kind way, was trying to discourage her ardor by avoiding her. Maybe he was just shy.

Checking her reflection in the hall mirror, Violet tucked stray hairs back into her bun, straightened the string tie at her throat, and bit her already rosy lips. Though she hated wearing black, this shirtwaist and skirt did accent her figure and the pearly sheen of her skin. Her hair was freshly washed. She had slept well the night before. On the whole she felt pretty, and this gave her self-confidence. *Hattie Thwaite, I intend to give you competition.*

She walked gracefully through the front doorway and down the steps.

Obie opened the garden gate. "Mornin', Mrs. Fairfield."

Violet smiled her brightest at him as she stepped through. "The same to you, Mr. Watson. It's a pleasure to see you again. Did you wish to speak with me?"

He suddenly pulled off his hat and fiddled with it, looking as shy and awkward as a boy. "I brought your horse. Heard you might be needing him."

Violet then noticed two horses waiting at the hitching rail,

Obie's homely paint and a strapping chestnut with a white snip on its nose.

"You brought me a. . . How did you know? Oh, you heard that I wanted a horse? My, but news travels quickly in this town. Um, thank you. I do appreciate it, honestly."

He just looked at her.

Flustered, she rattled on, "Well, I do need a horse—two, really. I guess it's obvious. . . How did you know I was planning to buy a team today?"

"I didn't know."

His unblinking regard began to irritate her. "Mr. Watson, would you please state your business and stop staring at me?"

He took a step back and donned his hat. "I didn't intend to be rude, ma'am. This is your horse, Barabbas." He indicated the chestnut. The animal took the opportunity to rub its sweaty ears against Obie's shoulder, but he shoved it away. "Remember? He belonged to. . .to Charles. You saw him at the house that day, when he came limping home. He's sound now."

"Oh!" she blurted, feeling gauche. "I. . .I forgot all about it. Is he gentle?" She reached out to touch the horse's face, but it jerked its head away, ears flattened, and snapped at the air with yellow teeth. Violet gasped, stepped back on her skirt's hem, and would have fallen if Obie had not caught her arm and hauled her back to her feet.

"Are you all right?"

Although he looked and sounded sincerely concerned, she yanked her arm out of his grasp and flashed, "I need a gentle animal, not a. . .a vicious beast!"

He blinked. "You can certainly trade him for a gentler horse, but I thought you'd want to make that decision."

She hung her head. "I'm sorry. I lost my temper at you again for no reason. You must think I'm an awful shrew."

He brushed the matter aside. "Do you know how to harness and hitch a horse?"

"I've done it before. If you think I can manage this one, I guess I'll keep him for now, but I would appreciate your. . . your advice while purchasing a vehicle. I've never bought one before. I don't know where to begin."

"What time?"

"I will leave in about half an hour. I need to arrange things with Amelia and the children."

"I'll wait, if you like, and you could ride with me to the livery stable. Irving should have some rigs to sell."

Violet glanced ruefully at the man's saddle atop Barabbas. "I'll walk. You were right about me not being a very good rider."

He looked abashed. "Forget I said that, ma'am."

"Perhaps I'll learn to be a better horsewoman under your tutelage."

"Mrs. Fairfield?" Obie doffed his hat again and fiddled with it, as if struggling for words.

"Please, after all we've been through together, I wish you would call me Violet."

He could not meet her eyes. "Violet, you look. . .mighty fine today," he stated. He then stalked to the hitching rail, released the horses, swung into Jughead's saddle, and rode away without a backward glance, shaking his bowed head.

Instead of hurrying inside, Violet stood in the open gateway and watched him out of sight. She liked Obie's square shoulders and small hips. He looked lithe and graceful on his horse. She liked his flat stomach and strong arms, and his beautiful gray eyes. . . Quickly she snapped the gate shut and hurried into the boardinghouse, hoping no one had seen her admiring the cowboy.

Later, at Irving's Livery, Violet listened and watched while the men tried a harness on Barabbas and haggled over the price. The horse objected to being harnessed. Violet's heart pounded when it kicked viciously at Obie, but he had seen the kick coming and moved out of range. Violet gasped when he calmly whacked the horse on the rump, but it subsequently allowed him to place the crupper under its tail. She had severe doubts about her ability to control this contrary beast even for a day or two.

When it came to choosing a vehicle, Violet was bewildered.

Irving showed her several conveyances, pointing out their high quality and good condition, but Violet had no idea which one would best meet her needs. She looked at Obie, and he quietly stepped in and chose a modest surrey for her, much like Amelia's but with a top that folded down. Its paint was faded and chipped, but the wheels and seats were good. "You need a surrey or rockaway for the extra seating. A buggy wouldn't hold your whole family."

"Will one horse be enough?"

"Barabbas is a powerful animal. He'll manage alone until we can find him a partner or trade him for a team."

To Violet's relief, Obadiah dickered the price down. She paid twenty-three dollars cash for surrey and harness. Obie shook his head over the exorbitant price, but Bill Irving acted as if he'd practically given the rig away.

Soon the surrey was hitched to her horse, and Obie lifted her to the seat. He tied Jughead behind and hopped up beside Violet, ready to drive. "You're coming with me?" she asked, unable to hide her relief.

"I don't know how well Barabbas drives." He picked up the buggy whip Irving had thrown into the deal and clucked up the horse. Barabbas tried to rear, but Obie quickly brought him under control. The surrey rolled into the main street at a reasonable pace. Violet held the seat with white-knuckled hands.

"What are your plans for the rest of the day?" Obie asked, maneuvering through traffic.

The horse's antics had crumbled her confidence. "I wanted to go to the house and start cleaning—maybe even move into it today. This morning I ordered supplies at Russell's, but they won't fit into this surrey along with the children. I guess I should have them delivered to my house. . . Oh, I don't know what to do next! Should I have purchased that wagon instead of a surrey? I don't know what I'm doing. Nick Houghton was right—I should just sell this house and go back where I came from."

"Why?"

Violet felt tears threatening, and this made her angry all over again. "Why? I don't know when to plant things or when to harvest them. I don't know the first thing about machinery or animals. I can't drive or ride well or even saddle a horse. I don't know how to repair anything except clothing. I. . .I only know that I love this place, and I want to belong here!"

"Is this where God wants you?"

"Do you mean, am I following His guidance? I don't know where else to go. I have no family still living. But what if I lose this house? What if we have to give it up because Charles Bolton's family comes to claim it? Then we would have to go back to Annapolis, and I don't like it there." She sounded slightly hysterical, even to her own ears.

"Violet, is Jesus Christ your friend?"

Violet calmed and looked at Obie. His hat was tipped back, and sunlight sparkled on the silver in his hair. His hair was thinning on top and she could see his scalp.

He glanced over, catching her in the act of staring. "Is He?"

She had almost forgotten the question. "Yes," she said quietly.

"He loves you the same as He ever did. You need to trust Him. He doesn't allow hardships or uncertainties without good reason."

Violet sighed. "I guess I've given Him lots of good reasons."

Undeterred, Obie continued, "When God sends a blessing, He expects His children to enjoy it, not worry that He will snatch it away again. He is our loving Father, not an erratic tyrant. Do you believe that He loves you?"

"Yes."

"Then you must know that He will care for you as He promised. He wouldn't take Jerry from you without providing for your future in another way. Remember the story of the lilies of the field and the birds of the air."

"He did provide an inheritance from my parents and the house from Jeremiah's parents, which is being leased and provides us with another source of income. But if we should lose this house and farm, I'm not sure my inheritance would last until the children are grown—and I have no trade, no means of earning a living. If I simply sit back and expect God to provide our needs. . ." Her voice trailed away. "The Proverbs revile a lazy and improvident parent."

"Are you lazy and improvident?"

She frowned. "I don't believe so, but it seemed to me that you recommended me to be so."

"Trusting in God is, therefore, lazy and improvident?" Obie halted Barabbas in front of Amelia's boardinghouse, but Violet was too absorbed in their conversation to notice.

"You insist upon twisting my words into things that I do not mean!" she snapped, turning to confront him face-to-face. "I am a good mother, and I try to put my children's welfare before my own. You are a bachelor, but surely you can understand my position. Jeremiah left us nearly five years ago, and I assumed leadership of the family, though I did not crave that role. I am now responsible to provide for my children."

"I disagree." Obie secured the reins and met Violet's glare.

"What possible grounds can you have for disagreement?"

"The book of James, chapter one, verse twenty-seven. Also, many other references that refer to the church caring for widows and orphans, as they cannot provide for themselves. As a believer in Christ, your brother in God's family, I am responsible to provide for your livelihood, as is every other Christian in this town."

Violet's pride was stung. All the while she had been daydreaming about him, he had considered her a charity project! She tried to sound nonchalant, but her voice revealed her hurt feelings. "And this is why you are help-ing me?"

"It's one reason."

Apparently considering the discussion at an end, Obie climbed down, tethered the horse, and came to assist Violet. She tried not to notice how his grasp on her waist increased her heart rate. Once on the ground, she brushed at her dusty skirts. "I thank you for your assistance. Good day, Mr. Watson."

He said nothing, but followed her inside. In the hallway, Violet stopped on the second stair and turned. Standing above him gave her the illusion of control. "I said 'Good day,' sir."

He nodded. "Yes, ma'am, you did." He tapped his hat against his leg.

"Is there something you need?" Violet tried to stare him down, but her eyes began to water. He was impossible to intimidate.

"Pack up and bring your children. I'll drive you out to the house; then I'll bring my wagon back to town for your supplies. Hurry." This said, he walked toward Amelia's kitchen.

Violet stared after him. His assumption of control irritated her, but she had to admit that his plan sounded ideal; she could potentially settle into her house this very night. A flicker of excitement banished her anger. Turning, she hurried upstairs in a hustle and bustle of skirts. "Beulah!"

seven

"Pure religion and undefiled before God and the Father is this,
To visit the fatherless and widows in their affliction,
and to keep himself unspotted from the world."
James 1:27

Samuel perched beside Obie, staring up at the man with evident adoration, listening and talking for all he was worth. Beulah and Eunice, on either side of their mother in the surrey's backseat, were also talking full speed, so Violet could hear little of the "man talk."

Satchels and valises were crammed in around their feet and Obie had promised to bring their trunk and other bags when he brought the supplies. Violet was still embarrassed by her dependence on his Christian charity, but at the same time she was thankful for his help.

Violet allowed herself to revel in the beauty surrounding her and promptly forgot her gripes and worries. *Lord,* she prayed silently, trying to block out the conversations around her, *I thank You for this beautiful place and for our beautiful house. You do bring good out of every situation, don't You?*

The surrey turned, and Violet recognized the overgrown lane. Her heart responded, pounding with anticipation. Was the house as wonderful as she remembered it?

Their ride was much smoother today. Someone must have filled in the potholes. Suddenly, the surrey lurched as the horse bounded forward. Their heads snapped backwards, and Eunice let out a terrified squeal.

"Whoa, boy. Whoa, Barabbas," Obie's deep voice soothed. He hauled the big horse down to an erratic trot, though the animal was evidently itching to run wild. Violet could see Barabbas's brown mane tossing and could hear his frenzied snorts. "Steady now. It was nothing to make you fly into a panic, boy."

"What happened, Uncle Obie?" Samuel asked, clutching his seat.

"A bird flew past his nose." Once the horse was under control, Obie turned his head. "You all right back there?"

"We're fine." Violet realized that had she been driving just then, they might all have been killed, for she could never have stopped the horse from bolting. Her arms were too weak. "Thank you."

At the house they all piled out of the surrey, grateful for solid ground under their feet. The girls looked pale and shaken, and Samuel blurted, "Mama, how are you going to drive this horse? He isn't quiet and gentle like you said you wanted."

Violet lifted a trembling hand to straighten her bonnet. Her eyes involuntarily flew to Obie's face. He looked serious, almost angry, as he said, "I'll look for a gentle team for you. In the meantime, don't try driving Barabbas anywhere."

Obie lifted two bags from the surrey and carried them up the steps. Violet and the children each claimed a bag and followed him into the house. "Let's just pile our things in the sitting room for the present," Violet suggested. To her amazement, the house was immaculately clean. All the clutter and destruction had been cleared away. The windows sparkled, the floors gleamed with wax, and the cobwebs had vanished.

"Oh, Mama, look!" Eunice pointed.

A pewter pitcher filled with flowers brightened the mantel. Violet reached high and lifted it down. She touched her face to a perfumed spray of lilacs. "This is lovely."

"Mama, it's clean in here, too, and someone left two pies on the table," Beulah called from the kitchen doorway. "They look like strawberry, my favorite."

"How very nice! Let's save them for supper tonight." Violet glanced around. "Obadiah, did you do all thi—?"

"He's taking the surrey around back, Mama. He left our stuff on the walkway."

"You all bring in the rest of our things; then you may head for your rooms and start unpacking. I'll find out what he's planning to do next. Get on with you now."

"Who cleaned the house and brought the flowers, Mama?" Eunice couldn't resist asking as she collected her satchel. "Do you think it was Mr. Watson?"

"Perhaps," Violet allowed. "But I'm pretty sure he didn't bake those pies."

Jughead was tethered to the hitching rail. With pricked ears and quivering nostrils, he watched Violet walk past. He looked friendly enough, though his blue eye had a glassy look. "Hello," she greeted. The horse shook himself, sending up a cloud of trail dust.

Violet hurried to the barn. The surrey was parked under an overhang. Obie had just finished hanging the harness on the barn wall. "Will that harness fit another horse?"

"If not, we'll trade for one that fits." He began to rub down Barabbas.

As he worked, Violet looked around. "This is a nice barn. Do you think we could keep a cow in here with the horses?"

"Yes."

Violet's eyes returned to Obie. His faded blue shirt had come untucked in places, though his suspenders strapped it against his trim body. The sleeves were rolled up above his elbows, revealing muscles that swelled and stretched as he worked over the horse. He must have removed his red combinations for the summer—his shirt's open neck revealed a strip of white undervest.

For the first time that day, Violet recalled Nick's accusations about Obie's past. Was he really a legendary gunman? Had he killed several men?

Obadiah Watson was certainly a strong, tough man, but she could not imagine him as a killer. Leaning against a post, she asked softly, "Obadiah, are you the one who filled in the potholes, cleaned up the house, and brought the flowers and pies?"

"Al, Myles, and I fixed the drive, but Caroline Schoengard

and Mamie Bristol did the rest. Like you said, word travels fast in this town." Violet could not read his face, for he was hidden behind the horse. He emerged a moment later, brushing his hands down his jeans, then led the horse past her and tied him in an open-backed stall. "I'll return with your things in a few hours. The horse'll be fine until then. I watered him already."

"Obie?" Her voice was low.

He paused in the barn doorway, but did not turn to face her.

"I want you to know that I'm eternally grateful. I don't know what I would have done without you today. I am certainly in need of Christian charity, and you have been more than kind. I'm sorry I shouted at you earlier." Violet twiddled her fingers nervously as she spoke. "I don't usually lose my temper so easily. I don't know what ails me lately."

She saw his chest expand in a deep breath. He said, "I'll be back," then continued outside.

Violet followed slowly, letting her eyes drift upward as she emerged from the shadowy barn into the sun-spattered freshness of the outdoors. Branches waved gently overhead, their leaves flashing from green to silver. In the woods beyond the house, Violet spotted the white trunks of birches among the stolid gray oaks, basswoods, maples, and elms.

Obie skidded Jughead to a stop before her and asked, "Thought of anything else you need while I'm in town?"

"As a matter of fact, I need two more blankets. Please have Mr. Russell put them on account for me. I will pay him as soon as possible. Thank you!"

Obie nodded and gave a short wave. Violet was startled when Jughead suddenly reared almost straight up, came down with a snort, and clattered away. She had heard that cowboys were amazing riders, but such a thing had to be seen to be believed.

As she ascended the front steps, the thought struck her that Obie had been showing off for her like a schoolboy for a girl he admired. She smiled, glancing back at the place she had seen him last, and felt her spirits rise. *Maybe he does like me more than a little.*

"Mama, I'm hungry." Samuel met her at the front door. "When are we going to eat?"

"In a few minutes. Mrs. Sidwell packed us a few things for dinner. When our supplies arrive, I'll cook us a hot meal. I ordered plenty of food."

"Do you know how to use this stove?" Beulah asked.

"It's much like the one in Grandma Fairfield's kitchen. Here's the water reservoir," she said, moving into the kitchen. "Here's the oven, and here's the firebox. Look, someone has put kindling in it, all ready to light. We might as well heat some water for coffee." She wanted to offer Obie a cup when he returned.

"I'll fill the kettle," Eunice offered, eager to try out the newfangled pump.

"Thank you, dear. Now, where are the cooking utensils stored?" Violet began to explore the kitchen cabinets. There was little to find. "I'll be thankful when our possessions arrive from the East."

"Did you send for them already, Mama?"

"I wired for them. They could arrive any day."

"I was so afraid you would decide to sell this house," Beulah admitted. "I saw Mr. Houghton after school one day, and he tried to make me ask you to sell. He told me all kinds of stories about how awful it is to live on a farm and about how much work we'd have to do."

Violet frowned. "Mr. Houghton doesn't know what is best for our family. Mr. Watson says that we need to accept and enjoy the gifts God sends and not worry. God will enable us to survive here, I'm certain."

"Uncle Obie says he'll teach me to be a farmer," Samuel announced, already chewing on a chicken leg he had sneaked from the basket Amelia had sent.

"Did he?" Violet smiled her pleasure.

"He says he'll teach me to fish, too."

"Samuel, you shouldn't call an adult by his first name," Beulah chided.

"All the kids call him that. He likes it," Samuel defended

himself. "I'm not being disrespectful. It's all right, isn't it, Mama?"

"If Mr. Watson doesn't mind, it's all right with me."

Eunice spread a cloth on the rough table, and Violet unpacked their dinner. "Mama, why does Mr. Watson help us like this?"

"He is trying to obey God's command that believers are to provide for widows and orphans."

"Isn't the church supposed to do that?"

"Mr. Watson tells me that many church members have pitched in to help us. Mrs. Schoengard and Mrs. Bristol cleaned the house, baked those beautiful pies, and brought the flowers. Wasn't that kind of them? Let's ask our blessing, children, before we talk anymore."

They held hands around the table as Violet quietly asked God to bless their food and their home. "Amen."

"Maybe he wants to marry you, Mama, like Mr. Houghton does."

Violet's eyes flew to her son's face. "What makes you say that, Samuel?"

"I heard some ladies talking in Mrs. Sidwell's parlor the other day while you were away. They said they would lay bets, if they were men, that he'd have you hog-tied within a month. They said he needs your money."

"Mr. Watson?" Violet felt a tightness around her heart.

"No, Mr. Houghton. They said he's a fortune hunter. Are we rich, Mama?"

The tightness eased into a relieved sigh. "Hardly. We have a tidy nest egg in the bank, but we are far from rich." Violet gave her son a steady look. "Why were you eavesdropping, Samuel?"

"I didn't mean to. I was in the broom closet, and its back wall leans up against the parlor. Once all those ladies arrived, I was afraid to move in case I knocked something over. Mrs. Sidwell threatened to flay me alive if I disturbed her Aiders' meeting. What does 'flay' mean?"

"I believe it means to skin something. No wonder you were

afraid to move." Violet smiled in spite of herself. "Please pass the carrots, Eunice."

❧

The family was outside making plans and exploring when hoofbeats sounded in the drive. Everyone hurried to greet Obie, but a lone horseman appeared instead. Violet and the children slowed to a disappointed walk.

"Howdy!" Nick Houghton shouted a greeting. His broad-shouldered physique made a striking picture astride a rangy bay. The sweat-drenched horse huffed noisily, drooping its head as soon as it stopped. Thick spume dripped from its mouth.

Nick swung down, tossed the reins around the rail, and approached Violet. "I heard about your move and made haste to offer my aid. Need help unloading supplies?"

Violet took a step back. Nick moved closer. She had to tip her head back to look him in the eye. "Our supplies have not yet arrived, but thank you for the kind thought."

"You know I worry about your safety, Vi, but I will try to restrain myself from voicing my doubts." He captured her hand and squeezed it until Violet thought her bones might break.

"Nick, please, my hand!" she exclaimed.

"So sorry, my dear. I hardly know my own strength." There was a strange light in his eyes—as though hurting her had given him pleasure.

He slapped his hat against his leg and looked around. "Got plans to rent out the fields? Could bring in a decent income that way."

"I have no plans at the moment. One thing at a time is all I can handle, and today I plan to move into my new home."

"Ah," was Nick's only reply. Violet studied his face while he studied the house. Nick's features were fine at first glance, but there was something missing. She wasn't sure which quality he lacked, but whatever it was, it was important.

"Someone's coming," he observed, turning away.

"It must be Mr. Watson with our supplies," Violet brightened.

At the sight of Obie on the seat of a loaded wagon, relief washed over her. She discovered that her hands had been balled into fists. Did Nick intimidate her so much? A moment ago he had casually demonstrated his vastly superior strength. If he wished to frighten her, he had succeeded.

Obie's pair of brown mules waggled their long ears when Samuel skipped, shouting, beside them. Obie hauled them in and leaped down, and Samuel gave the wiry cowboy an ecstatic hug.

"Uncle Obie, guess what we found? A whole nest of garter snakes! Mama says not to touch them, but I want to keep one. They were right alongside the toolshed."

"Better obey your mama, Sam. We'll get you a better pet than a snake. Come help me unload this stuff. We've got a mess of work to do here, and I need a man's help."

Obie nodded coolly to Nick and tipped his hat to Violet and the girls. "Please tell us where to put it all, ma'am." Then his eyes fell upon Nick's exhausted horse, and Violet saw a shadow of anger cross his face.

"Sam, before we start, how about you walk Mr. Houghton's horse till he cools, then give him a drink."

"Yes, sir." Eager to prove himself capable, Samuel pulled the gelding's reins loose and led him across the yard.

Violet couldn't help fluttering slightly, and Obie caught the anxious movement. "I know that horse, ma'am. He won't harm your boy. He's a fine animal. Too fine to be ridden hard and left standing in the hot sun."

Nick's face went white, and his lips almost disappeared. "What about your mules, Watson? Gonna leave *them* standing in the hot sun?"

"Sam will care for them next," Obie said. Lifting a covered bucket from the wagon bed, he turned to Violet. "Brought milk. I'll set it in the springhouse right off. We'll keep you supplied until you get a cow."

Nick swore outright. "What gives you the right to barge in here and distribute your second-rate largesse?"

Already on his way toward the creek, Obie turned to answer,

but Violet spoke first. "God gives him the right. He is representing the church body by caring for a widow in need, and I appreciate his help. He has given to us freely, just as the Lord provides for His own. Now, if you truly desire to be helpful, Mr. Houghton, you may begin by unloading those sacks of flour and sugar. I want them in my pantry. Beulah will show you exactly where when you get them inside."

Violet and Eunice unpacked some lighter items while Nick hoisted a hundred-pound flour sack up on his shoulder. Big man though he was, he seemed nearly crushed by the sack's weight. He staggered inside and dropped it heavily on the kitchen floor, panting like his winded horse.

"Oh!" Beulah exclaimed. "Watch what you're doing! You might have broken it, and then what a mess we would have. Please slide it over here against the far wall."

Violet hid a smile behind her hand at Nick's sulky expression. Rubbing his shoulder and grimacing, he poured himself a cup of coffee and relaxed at the table, watching while Obie brought in the other sacks and the trunk.

Samuel doggedly worked beside his hero, carrying in smaller items and placing them at Beulah's command. One word of praise from Obie was enough to make the boy's thin face glow with satisfaction.

At last the wagon was empty and the pantry was full. "Where did Mr. Watson go?" Violet brushed flour from her hands and removed her apron.

Beulah sprawled across a kitchen chair, her face smudged with flour. "I don't know. After he brought in that last load, he went back outside with Samuel. I heard him say something about cleaning up. Maybe he went home."

Violet's brow wrinkled. "Without a word to me? That isn't like him. Are the beans cooking?"

"Yes, Mama. I put in the salt pork, onions, and carrots just like you said. Eunice has to make the corn bread, doesn't she? I'm tired."

"You've done your part, dear. I'll handle the rest. Thank you so much!" Violet kissed the girl on her damp forehead and accepted a hug in return.

The kitchen door stood ajar, and Nick lounged against the doorjamb. "Excuse me, please," Violet requested, but he only drew on his cigarette, observing her through narrowed eyes. Beyond him she could see afternoon sunlight touching the treetops and casting long shadows over the barn.

"Mr. Houghton, please let me pass. You're blocking the doorway." Certainly she could have used the front door, but she was tired and cross and did not feel like going out of her way for this inconsiderate oaf.

"What will you do for me if I move?" Nick smiled slowly, his eyes begging her to respond in kind.

He was like an overgrown, indolent boy. She caught a whiff of his sour breath. "Ask me what I won't do. I won't kick you in the shins," she replied.

"Oh, darlin', you're just asking for a lickin'," he blurted gleefully and grabbed for her.

Violet's bravado instantly evaporated. She dodged and ran behind the table. "No! Truly, I'm not."

Eyes alight, Nick moved into the room, spreading his arms as though to sweep her in. "Come to papa, sweet thing."

As he passed, Beulah stuck out her foot and tripped him. He didn't so much as glance her way, but eased around the table, crooning to Violet as though he were wooing a frightened horse. Violet broke and ran for the open door.

Nick gave her a fair head start and watched as she raced across the yard with billowing skirts. Grinning, he flicked his cigarette to the ground and pursued her in earnest. From the doorway behind him, Beulah hollered, "Mr. Houghton, leave my mother alone!"

Obie must still be around. But where was he? In the barn? Hearing pounding footsteps, Violet dodged and doubled back toward the barn door. Nick's outstretched hand just missed snagging her flying skirts. She heard his boots skidding in the gravel, and he chuckled appreciatively.

What have I gotten myself into? When will I learn to watch my tongue? He thinks I'm flirting with him!

"Obie?" she gasped. "Obadiah, where are you?"

Nick grasped her arm and hauled her to a stop. "Now, what would you be callin' him for, honey gal? Thought you said he went on home. You trying to fool me?" There was an edge to his voice. "You and I are just having a romp. That old cowpoke will mind his own business if he knows what's good for his health."

A chill trickled down her spine at sight of his expression. "Mr. Houghton, please, I'm sorry if I've given you the wrong impression. I truly don't wish to romp. It's been a long day, and I'm very tired—"

"Females that trick a man thataway have only one thing coming to 'em," Nick announced, blue eyes sparkling. He swept her up into his arms and marched toward the chopping block, an old stump.

"No! Oh, please, Nick, let me be! This isn't funny! What will the children think?" Violet struggled vainly as he placed her face down across his lap. "Go away! Please go home and leave us in peace." Her voice crackled with anger and frustration.

He lifted his hand, but suddenly hauled her upright to sit upon his knee. Violet's breast heaved from her exertions, drawing his prurient eye. "You've got the wrong spirit about this, honey. Don't sound so angry and scared; you make a man feel like a heel!" Twisting one of her arms behind her back, he wrapped his arm around her waist and squeezed until her heart pounded against his ribs. "Mmm, that's better. You're such a sweet little thing that you make me forget all about your dignity. I just want to cuddle you close and soak you in."

He tried to nuzzle her neck. Violet squirmed her other hand free and beat at his chest, then pushed at his face. Shaking with fear and rage, she tried to sound authoritative, but her voice was tear-choked. "Mr. Houghton, I have no wish to be cuddled by you, so kindly remove that notion from your head. I am not a toy to be dandled on your knee and handled at will. Release me at once, do you hear?"

"You heard the lady, Houghton."

Nick's hands went limp. Violet wrenched away, lost her balance, and sat down hard in the dirt. Still gasping for breath, she lifted her eyes to see Obie standing just outside the open barn door. His eyes were glacial; his hands were alternately clenching and relaxing at his sides.

Nick seemed mesmerized by Obie's stare. Violet had never seen a man turn pale simply because another man glared at him. If she hadn't known better, she would have thought Obie was aiming a gun at Nick's heart. She jerked her gaze back to Obie; he held no gun. If he carried a weapon at all, it was not in evidence.

"Mr. Watson, we feared that you had gone. I. . .I want to invite you to stay for supper. It isn't much, but you're welcome to share it with us. You. . .I. . ." Her invitation sputtered to a sorry end. "Will you stay? Please?"

He glanced at her, and Violet thought she saw his eyes flicker with warmth. "I think it's time for Mr. Houghton and me to leave you. Perhaps another evening, Mrs. Fairfield." His eyes returned to Nick and frosted over again. "Houghton, give me a hand here, will you?"

Nick rose from the stump and slumped into the barn. A moment later he reappeared behind a battered wheelbarrow full of rotted boards and rusted, twisted metal. Obie supervised him closely. "Take it to my wagon and unload it into the bed."

Samuel followed the men through the barn doorway, carrying a sack that clanked whenever he dropped it, which happened about every third step. "Hi, Mama. Why're you sitting there? I got more horseshoes than you can shake a stick at!" he announced cheerfully. "Uncle Obie and me are cleanin' up a mess from behind the barn. I'm s'posed to put this junk into his wagon."

"Uncle Obie and I."

"Right. Why don't you come help Uncle Obie and I?"

"Uncle Obie and me, son."

"Mama, can't you make up your mind?"

She smiled weakly, tucking in her disheveled shirtwaist as

she struggled to her feet. "It's not my rule, dear. I'll explain it to you someday soon, but for now let me take one side of that sack and we'll carry it to the wagon together."

For once, Obadiah Watson was not working. His eyes followed Nick's every move, and he seemed tense, like a set bear trap. Violet sensed that there was more to this situation than she understood. She did not fear Obie, but she knew better than to distract him for the time being.

After Nick muttered a farewell, mounted up, and rode away, Obie seemed to relax. He and Samuel finished clearing rubbish from behind the barn; then they fed and watered Barabbas. Violet wanted a chance to talk with Obie alone, but the opportunity did not arise.

"Are you sure you won't stay for supper?" she asked as he climbed to the wagon seat. "There is plenty, and we would enjoy having your company."

Obie turned, met her gaze, but seemed lost in thought. Sensing an inner struggle, she batted her eyes, hoping to tip the scales in her favor. His eyes crinkled in the almost-smile that so attracted her. "Thank you, but I don't want to outstay my welcome. I'll check on you again soon or send Al."

Violet nearly pouted. "I wish you would stay."

"Why?"

One of the mules grew restless; Obie controlled it with a few twitches of his fingers on the reins.

"I. . .well, I like you very much. I enjoy your company, and I feel safe when you are near."

Without a word, he looked deep into her eyes. No longer icy, his gray eyes spoke volumes. As she read them, Violet's heart thudded against her ribs and her breath came short.

He opened his mouth as though to put his thoughts into words, but apparently changed his mind. Clucking to the mules, he quickly drove out of the yard, leaving Violet to stare after him, flushed in disappointment.

eight

"Knowye not that. . .ye are not your own? For ye are bought with a price: therefore glorify God in your body."
1 Corinthians 6:19–20

"Obadiah, I hear I've got competition as your best girl." Hattie interrupted his reading of a psalm to comment. "Talk is, you've got a handsome widow hanging on your arm these days, a Violet Something-or-other. Tell me about her."

Obie tried to hide his surprise. Had people been linking his name with Violet's? How would she react to this? His emotions churned into a discomforting mixture of pride, fear, and inadequacy.

"What do you want to know?" he rumbled, keeping his eyes on the text.

"Are you plannin' to wed the woman? I hear she's a recent widow, but some marry while in mourning, you know, especially when there are children to consider. She has three, right?"

He nodded. "Two girls and a boy. Beulah is sixteen, Eunice is twelve, and Samuel is not quite nine. Good children, they are."

"So you have a mind to become a father, have you?"

His face twitched.

"Why so pensive? You'd make a fine husband for any woman. I've often told Cyrus it's a cryin' shame that no woman snapped you up long ago, but then I guess you haven't been lookin' for a wife until now. You think she's pretty?"

Staring down at the open Bible, Obie nodded.

"Someone told me that she ain't above average, but perhaps it was sour grapes talkin'. I sure would like to see her for myself. Think you could bring her out for a visit? You've got to have my blessing, you know."

"Miss Hattie, I don't know that Violet wants me for a husband. I think maybe she just needs help, and I'm. . .available and willing. I'm homely as a skinned possum and nothing to attract a woman like Violet, unless she's desperate."

"But you'd take her any way you can get her?" Hattie guessed wryly.

Shamefaced, he admitted, "I got it that bad."

"Just because she's pretty? She'll be old and ugly someday, like me. You'd better have more reason than lust of the flesh for marryin' at your age."

One side of his moustache lifted. "I'll bring her to meet you; then you'll know. She's wonderful, Hattie. Sweet, kind, a good mother, hard worker, and she loves the Lord with all her heart. She loved her husband enough to follow him out here. . . ." He fell silent lest he reveal more than necessary about the real Jeremiah.

"I want to meet this woman afore I hand out any more advice. If she don't see what a prize you are, she ain't worth your time, honey. Any woman that'd marry a man just to keep her kids fed—"

"She's worth everything, Hattie. You'll see."

❧

Violet was doing laundry when Samuel's excited call reached her ears. "Someone's coming, Mama!"

Immediately Violet dropped Samuel's Sunday shirt back into the tub, dried her hands on her apron, ran to the door, ran back and removed her apron, ran back to the door, checking her hair and tucking in stray strands, and tried to compose herself by taking a long, quivery breath. Smoothing her hands down her skirt, she stepped outside to greet the guest.

It was Albert.

Violet extended her hand in greeting, concealing her disappointment that he wasn't Obie. "Hello again, Mr. Moore."

"Cousin Buck calls me Al, and I'd be pleased if you did, too." Albert gave her a charming smile as he took her hand. "Buck is helping out at the Updahls' and the Thwaites' today, so he may not have time to come here."

Violet's smile faded. Hattie Thwaite again?

"Hello, Al!" Coming from the barn, Samuel tried a hand-stand, but fell over backwards. Unabashed, he hopped up and hurried to greet the older boy.

Albert chuckled. "Hello, Samuel. You look happier than when I last saw you. Cousin Buck tells me you're a hard worker."

"Please come inside and have a drink, Al," Violet invited.

"Thank you, ma'am. Sam, thanks, but don't bother about my horse. She's in the shade, and she's not thirsty yet." Albert followed Violet into the house with Samuel at his heels. "Sure is good to see a family in this big house." He politely waited for Violet to join him at the table before sit-ting down. Sipping his water, he glanced around curiously.

"I haven't been off the farm much lately, but I've heard rumors that Nick Houghton wants to buy this place—or else marry you and get this place in the bargain. He's the type to seek a rich wife."

"But we're not rich! Mama says all we have is an egg in our nest," Samuel announced.

Albert shrugged and gave him a crooked smile. "You've got this place. You're rich enough even without an egg."

"I hope I can make enough profit from the farm to keep us all alive. I haven't any knowledge whatsoever about farm-ing," Violet confessed. Albert was only about seventeen or eighteen, but, like his cousin, he inspired trust.

"You don't need to farm, really. Sharecropping might be your best option. Cousin Buck mentioned that to me." Al drank the rest of his water and set the cup on the table. "Lease your land to farmers, then share in the proceeds from their harvest. It's simple." Then he smiled, his dark eyes twinkling. "Or you could marry a farmer and let him handle the work."

Violet fiddled with her cup. "Are there farmers in the area who might be interested? In sharecropping, I mean," she added hastily.

He grinned. "We could take on a field or two, and your neighbors on the west and north may well snatch up the offer.

You might also rent land for grazing. It won't bring as much, but it wouldn't have to be cleared and plowed. And I know one farmer who might be interested in that option. . . ."

Violet waved her hand in dismissal, trying not to smile. "Samuel dear, please go find your sisters. They may not know that Al is here. They're in the garden, I think."

"All right, Mama." Samuel gulped down the last of his water and ran outside, leaving the kitchen door wide open. "Beulah! Eunice!" his voice faded away.

Violet met Albert's candid brown eyes. "How long have you lived with. . .Buck?"

"Four years, ma'am. Ever since he quit the range and moved here. When he inherited his father's business, a mercantile in Los Angeles, he sold out, traveled east, and purchased the farm next to this one. I am my father's eldest son, but he has four other sons, so my parents didn't mind too much when I begged to leave California and join my cousin. I have always wanted to live in a land," he waved one long arm, "like this—where four seasons come in cycle, snow falls in the autumn and stays till the spring, and trees grow tall and thick. I like to hunt whitetails, not jackrabbits."

Violet warmed to the lanky boy. "Do you enjoy working for your cousin?"

"Very much. He's made me his partner. Since he spends a lot of time doing God's work, Myles and I do a lot of the farmwork. We don't mind. Buck's work is important to him and vital to the community. He works like a slave when he needs to, like when we sow or harvest, and he always does his share of the milking. He's also the handyman—he can fix anything."

"He's a wonderful man, isn't he?" Violet mused.

"You really like the old guy, don't you?" Al looked eager. "I was afraid the interest was on his side only. A woman could look a long time and never find a better man."

"So I've been told. . .repeatedly. Do you. . ." She stared at her twiddling fingers. "Do you think he is interested in marriage?" She wanted to ask about Hattie Thwaite, but couldn't think of a casual way to bring her into the conversation.

"He's never been interested before, but since you arrived, well. . .even Myles comments on how the boss dangles after you. Kind of like a moth to a candle, you know? The old man's smitten pretty hard, I tell you."

"He's not old," Violet protested.

Al's grin widened. "He's forty-two as of next week. Getting long in the tooth to think of marriage, though he can still whip me and Myles but good in a wrestling match. I'd be pleased if you two married; though it does seem strange. I mean, he's always been so shy of women."

From the corner of her eye, Violet spotted movement at the kitchen door. "Come in, girls, and greet our guest."

Albert rose and bowed. "I am honored to meet again the lovely Misses Fairfield." He lifted his eyes to their faces.

Violet almost laughed aloud. Her girls were evidently swept off their feet by such charm. Beulah, the practical and unromantic, actually fluttered her lashes as she curtseyed in return. Violet suddenly wondered how Beulah might look with her hair up. She was nearly seventeen, after all, and the long brown braids did look childish.

"Want to go down to the pond, Al?" Samuel invited.

"For a while, yes. I hear you want to learn how to fish."

"I sure do. Uncle Obie promised to teach me."

"Please be careful around the water, children." Al and the girls were really too old for such a reminder, but Violet couldn't help being a mother.

When the noisy chatter faded away, Violet stared out the window toward Obie's house. Her fingers tapped restlessly on the windowsill.

"Lord, am I wrong to feel this way?" she murmured aloud. "All I seem to think about anymore is. . .men. It seems so silly and childish—yet I can't help myself."

Ignoring the laundry that awaited her attention, she went to her room and picked up her Bible. Rubbing the worn, soft leather cover between her hands, she spoke aloud again. "I don't want to make a wrong choice. Lord, is it Your will for me to remarry, or am I being selfish and weak?"

Sitting on her blanket bed, she scooted back against the wall and opened the Bible. "As I recall, the apostle Paul gave instructions concerning widows in several places. Let me see." She ruffled through pages until she found First Corinthians seven. Reading avidly, she frowned. "Paul seems to think it best if a man never marries and a widow never remarries. Is my longing for a husband a sign of weak faith? I don't want to be divided in my loyalty to You, Lord, and I certainly don't want to come between You and. . .well, I'll be honest about this. . .between You and Obadiah. As a bachelor, he is free to serve others as You direct, but if he were married to me, he would be concerned about me and my children first."

She ruffled through more pages, arriving at First Timothy. "Now here Paul advises young widows—I hope I still fit into the 'young' category—to marry and have children lest they get themselves into trouble through idleness. I have known widows that ought to have remarried," she mused.

Looking up at the ceiling, Violet said, "Now here we have a quandary. An unmarried man is better off if he doesn't seek a wife. A young widow is better off if she marries. But how can she marry without causing an unmarried man to lose his bachelor status? Hmm? I wish I had Paul here; I'd give him a piece of my mind for being so ambiguous. I guess what I can gather from all this is that I need to pray for Your will, seek to glorify You, obey Your direct commands, then wait and see what happens. I promise not to be one of these widows that 'waxes wanton.' "

Violet prayed, opening her heart to the Lord about many matters. Afterward, feeling happy, content, and a bit guilty for neglecting her chores, she descended the stairs. Afternoon sunlight poured through the western windows, reminding her that curtain fabric needed to be a top priority on her next shopping list. Singing softly, she began to prepare supper, scrubbing a garment or two during free moments.

Lord, everyone assures me that Obie is interested in me; but then he spends so much time with this Hattie Thwaite. Does he intend to marry her? I could be misreading his intentions toward me. I also need to ask him about his prison record and hear the story straight. It's not right for me to drag information about him from everyone else.

While wringing out Beulah's chemise, she stopped and sighed toward the ceiling. "I'm doing it again, aren't I, Lord? Obie this, Obie that. Am I setting myself up for disappointment? Please give me wisdom in this matter."

Through the open door she saw Al and her children walk toward the front of the house, laughing and chatting like old friends. Al had stayed far longer than his original intent. His poor horse was undoubtedly tired of waiting for him.

Horse. Violet suddenly remembered Barabbas in the barn. Had anyone fed or watered that horse today? Drying her hands on her apron as she removed it, she hurried to the front door just in time to see Albert and his horse disappear into the trees.

Violet considered asking one of the children to care for Barabbas, but shook her head, recalling those pinned ears and wicked teeth. If anyone were to brave the horse's anger, it would be she. "Eunice," she called. "Please come watch the hash while I care for the horse. Samuel, I could use your help."

Barabbas squealed angrily as they entered the barn. "I'm so sorry," Violet crooned, slipping alongside him in the stall. She reached for his halter, intending to lead him outside. "I completely forgot about you. We're not used to having animals to care for."

The gelding flung his head up and crowded her against the wall. One of his big hooves ground into her foot. Violet let out a pained grunt.

"Mama, are you all right?" Samuel was frightened. "Why don't we just bring him a bucket of water?"

After pushing the beast off her foot, Violet ran from the stall. Barabbas was tied up, but his heels were free, and she had seen him try to kick Obie. "Good idea. Help me pump some, would you please?"

Some of the water spilled while she lugged the bucket inside, but there was plenty left. The horse allowed her into his stall and drank eagerly. Violet smiled, listening to him slurp and gulp. He paid no attention when she slipped away. "Samuel, dear, he must be hungry, too. Would you get him a forkful of hay?"

Samuel tried to fling the hay over into Barabbas's manger, but it kept hitting the top of the partition and falling back. "Let me try." Violet took the pitchfork from him, scooped up the hay, and gave a mighty heave. The hay landed on top of the wall.

"Watch out, Mama!" Samuel tugged on her arm, but he was too late. The hay fell back toward them, scattering over the floor.

"Whoever designed this barn was a dunderhead," Violet grumbled. Much of her hair had come unpinned and straggled into her face. Hay sprouted from her hair and clothing, making her itch unbearably.

Flushed and irritated, she had no choice but to go back into the stall with the horse. She raked up the hay and gathered it into her arms. Barabbas was eager to have the hay, snatching mouthfuls of it before she could stuff it into his manger. His cheek muscles bunched and relaxed right before Violet's nose. "Well, that wasn't so bad." She stroked his shining flank as she turned to go.

Then something struck her on the back, knocking her forward. With an involuntary shriek, she staggered out of the stall and landed on the wooden floor. On hands and knees she waited to catch her breath. There was a sharp pain in her back.

"Mama! What happened?" Samuel ran and skidded on his knees to her side. "Are you all right?"

"I think. . .I'm all right." Violet crawled forward, out of reach of Barabbas's heels, then braced one hand on the wall and looked back. The horse was still eating like. . .well, like a horse. He ignored her. Shock began to pass, and rage set in. Tears burned her eyes and overflowed.

Worried, Samuel touched her back. "Your dress is ripped, and there's blood."

Violet slowly stood up. "You stupid, horrid, vicious horse!" Her shaking voice rose in volume and pitch. "If I had a gun,

I'd shoot you right between the eyes, you nasty, rotten, ungrateful—"

A shadow fell through the open doorway. "Mrs. Fairfield?"

Violet's tirade concluded long before her anger was expended. She sucked in a noisy sob.

"Uncle Obie, Mama got hurt!" Samuel shouted. "Come quick!"

Violet heard quick steps; then Obie gripped her arms. "What happened?"

She didn't want him to see her in a rage, but her anger was still hot. Calming herself, she began quietly, "We were feeding the horse, and. . .Obie, you'll be angry with me, but I forgot all about him until a few minutes ago! Still, that's no excuse for—"

He slowly released her arms. His worried eyes took in her tears and her disheveled appearance. "Samuel said you were hurt."

"I put hay into the manger, and when I turned around something hit me on the back and knocked me down. He bit me and tore my dress!" She reached for her back with one hand, but couldn't touch the spot that hurt. Temper flared again. "He's a monster! You should just shoot him and save someone else the trouble." She shook a fist at the horse's backside. Barabbas's tail swished in total unconcern.

Obie whirled her around. "Excuse me, ma'am, but your injury should be checked. You've got buttons missing, and you're bleeding."

"I understand. Go ahead." Violet reached up to pull her tangled hair out of the way. For the moment, she was too upset to care about modesty. Tears still trickled down her cheeks, and she was helpless to stop them.

"You want *me* to. . .to. . . ?" he stuttered, dumbfounded. He cast a helpless look at Samuel.

"What's wrong, Uncle Obie?" Samuel asked. "Mama's mad enough to shoot *Barabbas,* not you."

"I. . .uh. . .can you unbutton those top buttons, Sam? My. . . uh, fingers aren't so good at it."

"I'll try." Samuel unbuttoned the top few buttons of his mother's dress. "I'd call Beulah, but she'd probably faint. She can't even take a splinter out of my finger without getting sick." He pulled the fabric aside to expose the injury. "Ooh, yuck!"

"What?" Violet gasped.

Obie's voice was tight. "It's a nasty bite."

"Is it bleeding much or just bruised?" Violet tried to reach over her shoulder and touch the sore place, but she couldn't reach from that direction, either. She turned around just in time to see Obie disappear through the doorway.

"Where is he going?"

"He pulled out a handkerchief. I bet he went to get it wet. Mama, that bite looks nasty. There's a big purple ridge and teeth marks. It's disgusting!"

"He got me right between the shoulder blades. I never could reach that spot." She reached an arm back and tried to touch the spot from beneath, but felt only the edge of her chemise. How embarrassing! But it was a clean one, trimmed with lace, and at least that stupid horse hadn't ruined it. She wiped her sleeve across her face, but new tears replaced the ones she wiped away.

"Mama, if you don't need me anymore, I want to go outside for a while. May I check on my robin's nest?"

"I'd rather you stayed here for a few more minutes." She gulped on another sob. As her anger ebbed, a feeling of weakness took its place. She felt exposed and distressed.

"You're gonna have a big bruise, I bet." Samuel poked at his mother's back, and she flinched.

"Hey, be gentle, Sam." Obie appeared, holding a damp handkerchief that was folded into a pad.

"I didn't touch the bite," Samuel defended himself.

Obie gently gripped Violet's shoulder. "This will be cold," he warned, and pressed the pad upon the bite.

Violet gasped. Trying to hide her reaction to the pain, she asked, "Is it still bleeding?"

"A little. You should soak it in Epsom salts and paint it with iodine when you get the chance."

"I like putting iodine on cuts," Samuel said, watching closely.

"No, you don't. Not on your own cuts," Violet tried to chuckle, but the attempt was weak. Everything about her felt feeble.

Obie was gentle with the cloth. "Let's get you inside where you can sit down, Violet."

"All right." Appreciating his tender care, she laid her hot, damp cheek against his hand. "Thank you."

"Does it hurt very much?" His soft voice made her feel like crying again.

"Not terribly much. I just feel so. . .so weak. Don't know why I'm such a ninny. I'm not mortally wounded."

"You've had a shock. Here, take my arm, and we'll head for the house. The girls can get you cleaned up. Someone needs to take care of you, for certain."

Violet gratefully wrapped both hands around his arm and leaned her head against his shoulder. "You're doing a good job of it."

"May I go now, Mama?" Samuel fretted, bored with the proceedings.

"All right. Don't go far; supper should be nearly ready."

"Can you make it to the house, do you think?" Obie asked, concerned, as they reached the open barn door.

"I'm sure I can. I'm not *that* badly hurt." Violet tipped her head back. "You're such a dear!" Rising on tiptoe, she pressed her lips to his cheek and heard him inhale sharply.

"Mama!" Beulah stood just outside. "What are you doing?"

nine

"By love serve one another." Galatians 5:13

Facing her outraged daughter, Violet quietly said, "Mr. Watson has been very kind. I simply kissed him on the cheek."

Beulah frowned, her dark eyes taking in her mother's unkempt appearance and Obie's obvious discomfiture. "We have company. Didn't you hear the horse outside?"

"No, I didn't. Who is it?" Her unbuttoned dress suddenly slid down her shoulder; she pulled it firmly into place with her free hand.

Caroline Schoengard stepped into view. "Hello, Obie. Didn't mean to take you unawares, Violet. I brought over some vegetables from our garden."

"How kind of you! Mr. Watson was just helping me with the horse. He bit me right on the back—the horse did, I mean," Violet stammered. She felt hotter than ever, but she recovered her dignity enough to shake her visitor's hand.

The pastor's wife looked as though she might laugh. "I see. Are you all right?"

"I think so. It hurts some." Violet's tears brimmed again.

"It needs to be looked after right away," Obie stated bluntly. "I'm glad you're here, Caroline." He took hold of Violet's shoulder and turned her to show Caroline her back. Violet let her face rest against his chest for one blessed moment.

Caroline sobered immediately. "Oh, Violet, I'm so sorry! Obie's right; that needs immediate attention. I've got time to stay a spell. Ma Schoengard is keeping the boys for me again and fixin' supper."

Violet wanted to stay right where she was, but she lifted her head and moved away. "Thank you, Caroline. Please join us for supper."

Caroline took Violet's other arm, and Obie released her. She wasn't sure whether or not she should invite Obie to join them, but he made the decision for her.

"Good evening, ladies. I'll take Barabbas to my place until I can trade him off."

"Obie, thank you again—and tell Al thank you for the milk he brought. We enjoyed having him here today." Violet tried to smile normally.

Obie grumbled something.

"Pardon?" Violet asked.

"He was supposed to care for your horse while he was here." He headed toward the barn, looking like a thundercloud.

Beulah took her mother's other arm and whispered, "Mama, I'm sorry I shouted at you. I didn't know. . ."

"I understand, and you're forgiven." She squeezed the girl's arm. More tears poured down her cheeks. In her present mood, everything seemed to make her cry.

Obie led the wild-eyed horse from the barn. The ladies stopped for a moment to watch. Barabbas snorted, lunged, and did his best to escape, but Obie quieted him with a firm hand and a low command. "Should never have left you here. What was I thinking?"

Holding the lead rope, Obie mounted his paint. "Ma'am, Mrs. Schoengard, Miss Beulah." He tipped his hat to each lady in turn, then rode away with Barabbas trotting behind.

❧

Violet lay face down on her bed of blankets, since her actual bed hadn't arrived yet, and winced as warm water trickled down her sides. Caroline had found Epsom salts among Violet's supplies and was serving as self-appointed nurse. "I'm sorry to get your bed wet, my dear. You have other blankets, I hope?"

"Yes, we do. Don't worry about it. It just tickles, that's all."

"You'll be sore for a few days, I'm sure. You're really more bruised than cut, which is good. Less chance for infection to get into your skin." She shifted her seat on the "bed," groaning, "How can you sleep on this? I wouldn't be able to move in the morning."

"It's not that bad once you get used to it. Besides, I just received word that our furniture and other baggage should be arriving early next week. I'm so excited!"

"I'm sure nearly everyone in the area will want to help you bring it home and set up house. We can give you a proper housewarming then. Your moving here took everyone by surprise—we hardly did a thing to help out."

"But," Violet protested, "the pies, the flowers, and all the work that was done around the house to prepare it for us—I would call that quite a lot. We felt very welcomed indeed!"

Caroline smiled. "Oh, honey, just you wait. We'll have a proper shindig for you. I'll spread the word around. Not a dance this time, although you do have the ideal front room for it. We'll just have a party while bringing in your fancy things."

"Not so fancy, really, but they mean a great deal to me. I have many pieces that belonged to my parents. They've been in storage for years, since we've been living at my in-laws' house."

Caroline lifted the cooled compress and replaced it with a warm one. "Why didn't you move out here with Jerry in the first place? He never mentioned his family. Folks were mighty surprised when you showed up here."

Violet wriggled, irritated by her soggy chemise. "They were surprised?"

"Lots of folks scratchin' their heads. Jerry was a good man in his way, I'm sure, but. . .well, you're a handsome and refined lady, and. . ."

Violet studied the wall, noting cracks in the plaster. "It's hard to explain, Caroline. In fact, I can't really explain it all right now; however, I think the truth will come out in good time."

Caroline laid a sympathetic hand on Violet's arm. "You don't have to tell me, you know, if it's painful for you. I'm just a nosy woman who asks too many questions. Now, Violet, I'm going to dab iodine on your cuts, so prepare yourself."

Violet clenched her teeth, but couldn't wait to answer. "Caroline—ouch! You don't understand. I was very happily married, but that seems like a lifetime ago. Oooh! I wish I could tell you, but I can't yet. Please, Caroline, you don't need to feel sorry for me. It isn't necessary. Except for this iodine, I'm not in any pain."

"Well, maybe now you're ready to begin a new life," Caroline decided, replacing the bottle's stopper. "I hope and pray that you'll find it here, Violet." She grinned. "You now have a purple blotch that contrasts fetchingly with your lovely white skin. By the way, I couldn't help seeing that kiss today. Maybe my matchmaking prediction wasn't so far off after all."

Violet rolled her eyes. "I simply kissed his cheek. Samuel was with us until a moment before you arrived. It wasn't as improper as it must have looked. I don't understand why Beulah flew into a frenzy. I thought she knew me better than that!"

"She was playing the part of mother, I think. It did look suspicious, you two coming out of the barn with your untidy condition and unfastened dress. I think she reacted before she thought it through, that's all."

"And what do you think? Was I. . .out of line to kiss him like that?"

"We—ell, he is a bachelor, and. . .quite susceptible."

"You're right. At my age, I should know better." Violet felt tears threatening again.

"Are you in love with him, honey?"

"I. . .I think I may be. . .learning to love him."

Caroline's blue eyes looked troubled. "I could tell you a few things about him, but I don't want you to get the wrong idea. I mean, some of the things I know sound bad, but Obie is. . .well, he's simply a good man. David thinks the world of him. Our boys adore Obie, and he is wonderful with them."

"He loves children. I don't think you could tell me anything that would lower my opinion of him, to be honest. Obie is gentle and kind—he's no killer, I'm sure!"

"Violet, I think you ought to know that some people believe Obie was involved in your husband's death—because of his past record, you know. No serious accusations have been made, for there is no proof or real motive—but the talk is out there. If you were to marry Obie, it might increase."

"He had nothing at all to do with Jeremiah's death. I know

that for a fact."

"I'm glad to hear it, Violet. He deserves your faith in him, I'm sure."

There was a knock at the door, and Eunice pushed it open with one foot. "Supper is served. We decided to bring it up to you, since Mama can't come down."

"I probably could have come," Violet protested, "but thank you for the thought. Just set it on the floor here, and I can reach it."

Eunice glanced at her mother's back and made a face. "Poor Mama! Beulah told me what happened. I'm glad Uncle Obie and Mrs. Schoengard were here to take care of you. I wouldn't have known what to do, and Beulah says she felt faint just from looking at your back." She arranged the steaming plates on the floor and handed two napkins to Caroline.

"Wish I could see it," Violet grumbled. She lifted her face to accept a kiss from the girl. "Supper smells wonderful, dear. You're becoming an accomplished cook."

When their plates were cleared, Caroline gathered them up and stood. "I hate to leave, but I don't want to drive home after dark. Oh, before I forget, I mentioned your idea about a 'Care Committee' to David, and he really likes the idea. I imagine he'll mention it to Obie."

Violet gingerly sat up, holding her chemise and blanket to her chest. "Thank you for all the help, Caroline. I don't know what we would have done without you."

"God sent me today, I'm sure. Now you stay put and rest for a while, do you hear?" Caroline eyed Violet narrowly. "How'd you keep such a fine figure after three children, anyhow? My figure went to pieces after the twins, and I can't seem to get it back together."

Violet's smile was slightly crooked. "I got pretty hefty a few years back, but I realized I only made myself depressed when I couldn't fit into my clothes. I stopped eating so many sweets, and I work hard around the house. That's all."

"It's just not fair. Guess I'll hafta love you anyhow."

"You'd better."

ten

*"With all lowliness and meekness,
with longsuffering, forbearing one another in love."*
Ephesians 4:2

"Mama, guess what!" Samuel burst into the house, leaving a trail of dirty footprints. His jacket and trousers were filthy, but his face was beaming. A strong fishy odor filled the kitchen.

"What, dear?" Violet restrained a gasp of horror lest she dash his joy. She laid aside her mending and caught the boy before he could do further damage to her floor.

"I caught seven fish, and five of them are big enough to eat. Uncle Obie helped me scale and gut them. Would you cook them for supper tonight?" Samuel was ecstatic. Violet could not recall ever seeing the boy more thrilled.

"That's wonderful, Samuel! Yes, I will cook them, and I'm sure they'll be delicious. Now I want you to take a bath. I'll call Beulah to fill the tub, and afterward you will put on some clean clothes. Is Mr. Watson still here, or did he leave?"

"I think he's still around. Why can't my bath wait until after supper, Mama? I want to tell him good-bye."

"Bath first. Maybe he'll stay for supper; I'll go ask him. You start getting ready for your bath." She found Beulah in her room, piecing a crazy quilt with scraps from Eunice's cast-off dresses. "Honey, please draw Samuel a bath—I want to invite Obie to supper tonight and I've got to catch him before he leaves."

Without waiting for a reply, she clattered downstairs and out the front door, her heart racing. Jughead stood waiting at the hitching rail, saddled and ready to go, but dozing with one hind leg cocked. Violet bravely patted his shoulder in passing.

111

"I'm glad to see you're still here." After that painful bite, she was more wary of horses than ever, but Jughead was different. He belonged to Obie.

She found Obie bent over the outside pump, sluicing slime from his fishy hands. "Obie, I'm glad you're still here! Please—"

The noise of running water drowned her voice, and at the sight of her, he interrupted, "Mrs. Fairfield, I'm sorry Samuel is so dirty. There was little I could do to clean him up short of dunking him under the pump—"

She shouted, "Oh, don't worry about that; I've seen worse. Please stay for supper tonight and sample some of Samuel's fish. He would be very pleased." The water slowed to a quiet trickle, and her voice lowered to match it.

He looked tempted, but glanced down at himself. "I'm not so presentable myself, ma'am." Fish scales sparkled among the dark hairs on his forearms. Every exposed inch of his tanned skin glistened with sweat, which had trickled through dirt on his temples, leaving muddy streaks. He smelled, if possible, worse than Samuel.

"Couldn't you clean up and come back? We've hardly seen you this week. I would love to cook a nice meal for you." Violet stepped closer and saw his eyes dilate.

"If you're sure," he wavered.

"I'm very sure. I've wanted to have a good talk with you—I mean, to get to know you better. You're always so busy, and. . .well. . ." Violet started to flounder. "It seems as if you visit Hattie Thwaite nearly every day. Is she. . .I mean. . .I need to know, do you. . .are you. . .sweet on her?"

Obie's startled expression softened into a wide smile, showing his slightly crooked white teeth. "I sure am, but she's already taken."

"Taken?"

"She and Cyrus celebrated their fifty-eighth anniversary in March. You know Cyrus from church, don't you?"

"I. . .I never heard his last name," Violet faltered, feeling her face grow hot.

"I just sit with her and help out around their farm sometimes. If you like, I'll take you to meet her. Hattie has been asking to meet you, and Cyrus loves children."

"I see. I would. . .I would like to visit them." She could not meet his gaze and turned to flee.

"Wait, Violet," he spoke softly. "Don't be embarrassed. I'm glad you asked me. I like it that you're direct. I like. . .most everything about you."

Violet paused and lifted tear-wet eyes. "But I'm so. . .I've been chasing you like a. . .a wanton widow!"

"It's a new experience for me, being chased by a beautiful woman. I don't have much of a mind to run, so be careful you don't catch something you'll want to throw back." His eyes looked dark and suddenly serious.

She nodded, unable to speak.

"I'll be back for supper."

She nodded again, stiffly.

"Are. . .are you sure you want me to come back tonight?"

This time she smiled weakly and nodded.

&

Standing in front of the wavy old mirror, Obie straightened his string tie and stared critically at his reflection. He had never been one to care about his looks, but tonight his ordinary appearance annoyed him. "Wish You could have seen fit to gift me with a few more inches and pounds, Lord," he sighed. "I do look scrawny as a plucked banty rooster and about as handsome. Not a likely match for a blue-eyed beauty."

He didn't dare voice the thought aloud, but he wondered if Violet could possibly endure his touch, let alone enjoy it. His rough, scarred hands against her white skin? Even the thought of it started a fire burning within him, and he winced, knowing he should not allow himself to entertain impossible dreams. Grimly he forced the memory of her smooth white back out of his thoughts. Yet he possessed one memory that could be cherished always—the touch of Violet's lips upon his cheek, a gift she had freely given.

Obie looked into his reflection's eyes and shook his head.

"Was she really jealous of Hattie?" A smile lifted the corners of his moustache. "Maybe I do have a chance, after all."

Before riding away, he checked on Treat's pups. The fuzzy babies no longer stayed inside their box, but wandered around the tack room. They bounded to greet Obie and yipped their delight. "Where is your mother? Deserted you again, has she?"

Treat now took every opportunity to escape her motherly duties and catch a few moments of uninterrupted sleep. Obie had already sighted her, curled up on a fallen horse blanket just outside the calves' stall.

"Poor li'l tykes, left all alone in here to pillage and destroy." A well-chewed bridle strap caught his eye, and he sighed, shaking his head. He hoped Violet would forgive him for inflicting one of these destructive little creatures upon her household; he intended to present Samuel with a pup as soon as they were old enough to leave their mother. For several minutes he patted roly-poly little bodies, scratched a freckled tummy, and stroked soft ears, yet they still protested when he left them.

"Soon one of you will get all the attention you want," he promised. He could already picture Samuel with a fuzzy pup in his arms. That boy needed a good dog.

Back at Fairfield's Folly, Obie unsaddled Jughead and loosed him into the paddock. The delightful aromas emanating from the house made his mouth water. It had surprised him to learn that Violet could cook. She seemed like the type of fine lady who would have kept servants.

The door opened for him before he could knock. "Good evening, Mr. Watson," Beulah said formally and dropped a curtsey.

Obie pulled off his hat. "And to you, Miss Fairfield."

Then Eunice appeared in the doorway. "Hi, Uncle Obie! Come on in and make yourself at home. Mama outdid herself tonight. We've got fish and corn bread with honey and jam, fresh greens and cooked carrots and two pies for dessert! Do you like cream on your pie? Al brought us some this morning along with the milk and eggs. He and Beulah sat in the parlor and talked until it got too hot to stay indoors."

"Is that so?" Obie grinned at the girls, surprised to see Beulah's olive cheeks flush. He had not realized that a youthful romance might be brewing under his very nose. "Sounds like quite a feast. So your mama is a good cook, is she?"

"The best. Father's friends used to invite themselves over for dinner sometimes, but Mama never minded. She likes to cook for people who like to eat."

"Then she'll like cooking for me." Obie hung his hat on a wall peg. The house was warm, though every window stood open to catch the evening breezes. A fly buzzed in lazy circles around the entry hall. "Where's Samuel?"

"Still bathing. He wouldn't get himself clean, so Mama took over scrubbing his neck. He still stinks of fish, but you don't. You smell nice. Is that cologne?"

"Not too strong, is it?" He asked, rubbing at his freshly shaven neck. "Al said ladies like it."

"This lady does. I can't smell it unless you're close by."

Beulah had allowed her sister to do all the talking, but now she put in a question. "Al uses cologne?"

"No, he doesn't. I've had this stuff for a long time, but never used it before. I can't even remember where I got it. Maybe from Hattie or another lady at the church."

"Would you like some water? We have no ice since we just moved here, but our well water is cool."

"Yes, thank you. Sounds good."

Eunice went to fetch the drink. Beulah finally offered, "Want to come into the kitchen and sit down? We haven't any chairs besides the kitchen chairs and benches."

"Sure."

Violet entered the kitchen from the laundry room a few minutes later, wiping her hands on her black taffeta skirts and leaving long water streaks. She apologized for being late, and instantly put the girls to work serving supper. Samuel sulked in, looking freshly scrubbed, his dark hair plastered against his head except for one stubborn tuft on top. He cheered quickly at the sight of Obie.

"Did you empty your bathwater?" Violet asked. Samuel hadn't, so Obie volunteered to help him. They dumped the tub beside the back door to water the hollyhocks.

The family talked as they prepared to eat, including Obie in their discussions. He watched Violet as she moved about the kitchen, realizing that she had dressed up for the occasion. She had styled her hair in a fancy way, with curls dangling here and there. Her rustling gown was almost skintight in the bodice, with what looked like an immense pile of cloth drawn up to perch at the back of her hips. Her trim waist and full bosom rose gracefully from this virtual mountain of cloth. Obie thought it an odd style, yet he felt that Violet would look fabulous in almost anything.

Flies and yellow jackets buzzed about the dining room, attracted by the aroma of fried fish. Everyone fought to keep them off the food. Violet asked Obie to offer thanks, which he did in his quiet way. After the "Amen," their eyes met across the table, and she smiled, increasing his heart rate.

All three children tried to dominate the conversation.

"Mama, Clementine's brother William told Sybil's brother Hank that he wanted to ask me to the basket social they have every fall to raise money for school functions. I think he's very handsome, but I don't like the way he flirts with every girl he talks to." No longer stiffly silent, Beulah talked whether or not anyone listened.

"I wouldn't like that either, dear. It's a little early to be thinking about fall functions, don't you think? Eunice, please don't hum at the table. Yes, I do like your singing, but it's not polite to sing at the table; you know that. Now, what did the fish do, Samuel?"

"This one stole Uncle Obie's bait twice before he hooked it and let me reel it in. We could see it under the water. I tell you, this fish was mighty powerful. It made my rod bend, and I thought I lost it once, but Uncle Obie helped me get its head up and keep it away from snags. He had to dig the hook out of its throat with pliers, 'cuz it swallowed the worm right down, and his hands got all bloody. It flipped and struggled in the creel for a long time before it died, too."

Eunice gagged on the bite she had just put into her mouth. Covering her lips with a napkin, she choked until Beulah thumped her on the back. "Oh, Samuel," she groaned. "Don't talk about how a fish died while we're eating it. That's horrid!"

"Mama, please make him stop," Beulah joined in. "It's so ungenteel."

"All right now, you children be quiet and eat politely for a while," Violet decreed. "Whatever happened to 'Children should be seen and not heard'?"

Obie hid a grin with his napkin. He met Violet's apologetic eyes and shook his head slightly to indicate that he didn't mind them. She smiled in relief and gave him a helpless little shrug.

Perspiration dotted Violet's upper lip and made her smooth forehead shiny, but Obie thought he had never seen anyone more lovely. The supper was as delicious as promised, and the pies! Obie had a slice of each, shoofly and custard, with plenty of cream.

The girls cleared the table, but Obie insisted on helping with cleanup duty, wiping dishes and putting them away at Eunice's direction. Once Violet backed into him, her voluminous skirt engulfing his legs. He nearly dropped a tin plate.

"Excuse me, Obie. This isn't the most practical of gowns for daily life, but I get so tired of my plain black skirts. I wore this to my parents' funeral—they were well-to-do, and I needed a stylish gown. I haven't had any use for it since, however."

"Mama, you look like a dream in it, as you well know. All that taffeta!" Beulah chided her parent.

"All that fabric must weigh a lot. I don't see how you can stand wearing that rig in this heat," Obie commented.

Violet looked hurt. "It isn't that heavy, and the taffeta breathes easily."

A strained silence followed. The girls hung up their dish towels and left the room, chatting casually.

"Violet," Obie gripped her arm gently. "I didn't intend to hurt your feelings. You do look. . .like a dream, as Beulah said. I'm not one to appreciate style, I guess, but you always look just fine to me."

She gave him a prolonged view of her thick lashes before lifting them to display her stunning eyes. He released her arm and swallowed hard.

"Thank you. I need to learn which styles you do admire. We know very little about each other, really."

"I'll do my best to answer any question you want to ask."

"Isn't there anything you want to learn about me?"

Obie felt the tide of red creep up his neck again. "Yes, many things."

"Come, let's sit down at the table and I'll pour the coffee. Would you like more pie?"

"No, thank you. It was great though. Best I've ever eaten, I think. Where did you learn to cook?"

"My mother taught me. She believed that every woman should know basic housekeeping skills. It was a good thing, for Jeremiah and I could never afford to pay a cook. I always cooked for our family." Violet poured amber coffee into the two cups.

"Not only beautiful, she can cook!" Obie smiled bashfully, turning his cup between his rough hands and studying the steam.

Violet sat beside him in Samuel's chair. "Do you think I'm beautiful? I realize that true beauty comes from within, but I have always wanted to be pleasant to look at."

"Surely your husband told you how lovely you are. A man would have to be blind not to see. . ." He lowered his eyes back to his cup, afraid of saying too much.

"Thank you," Violet breathed, her eyes alight. "I know you'll think I'm vain, but I try so hard to look my best. It is good to know that you. . .approve."

"How's your back?"

Wondering about his train of thought, she answered, "Healing nicely. Caroline nursed me well. I still feel stiffness if I bend over or reach my arms up, but it doesn't hurt anymore."

"Did you want to ask about my past?" Again, Obie abruptly changed the subject.

"Yes, if you don't mind. I've heard several versions of your story, but I want to hear it from you. I know that you were accused and convicted of robbing a gold shipment and that you were in prison at a place called Yuma. The sheriff told me that much."

"What else have you heard?"

"Nick Houghton told me some nasty things about you, but I considered the source and disregarded everything he said. I can't believe that you killed anyone, let alone shot a man from a running horse like he said you did."

Obie straightened abruptly. "Houghton said he had *seen* me shoot a man from a running horse?"

"Yes. . .well, he intimated that he had; then he dropped the subject when I questioned him," Violet said, puzzled by Obie's reaction, "so I assumed he was making it all up. He said that you shot a man from a running horse while lying on your back. Is that even possible?"

"Nick Houghton. Could it be?" Obie mused quietly.

"*Have* you shot a man on a running horse?"

"Only once."

"While lying flat on your back?"

"Yes."

"And killed him? You really have killed people?" Violet gulped.

"Yes, I really have. Not for many years, but I have killed at least five men and wounded many others. I'm not proud of that fact, but it's the truth."

"During the war?"

"No, I was in prison during the War Between the States. Before that I worked as a hired gun for a time, along with Boz. We fought in several battles against Indians or outlaws. I've never killed in cold blood or in anger, and I haven't shot anyone since Yuma, since I became a believer. The last man I killed was Edwin Bolton, the older brother of the man who impersonated your husband."

"Oh!" Violet's voice was small. Each time he said the word "killed," a knife pierced her soul.

"I was imprisoned for Edwin's murder and for the murder of the men who carried the gold shipment. Edwin and his two younger brothers had stolen the gold and killed the four guards. I was too late upon the scene to save those men, but I shot Edwin as he tried to escape. Problem was, he had already shot my horse and got me in the leg, so I couldn't chase the other two or leave the scene. I was found there the next day with the five bodies and no gold. The two remaining Bolton brothers claimed that they had surprised me committing the crime. Although the gold was never found, it was assumed that I had stashed it somewhere. It was my word against theirs, and their father was important in that community. I didn't stand a chance, no matter how improbable their version of the story sounded. Except for one godly man who pled my cause, I would have been hanged for a crime I didn't commit."

"Oh!" Violet's eyes were enormous.

"That man came faithfully to visit me in prison. I was bitter at first, naturally; but, after a year or two, God softened my heart. I prayed with Burt to receive Christ, and he discipled me for two more years until his death. Burt Squires had never been strong, and the desert heat finally killed him. I missed him something awful, but after he died, I started sharing my faith with other prisoners and the prison guards, and before long there was a group of us that met together to pray and study the Scriptures. It was a great place to grow in grace and knowledge of my Lord and Savior." Obie smiled, though his eyes held a hint of sadness.

"How long were you there?"

"Ten years."

"Ten years!" Violet mouthed the words in sympathetic horror.

"After my release, I went back to being a cowhand, hiring out with a cattle outfit in the Rockies. I met up with Boz Martin, who had become a lawman. I told him my story and asked for his help; he told me about my father's death. So, I traveled back to California, sold Dad's business, and brought Al with me out here. We settled here because one of Boz's friends, a federal marshal, had given him a tip that one of the Bolton brothers had been seen near this area. I'd been praying for years that God would somehow clear my name, and this seemed like part of His answer. Al and I bought a farm and settled down; Boz got the job as Longtree's sheriff. Problem was, I didn't recognize Charles after so many years. Lived and worked right near the man and never knew him."

"Did he have the gold?"

"We think so. He wrote a letter before he died, but we couldn't read it. Boz sent it off to be analyzed, and we hope it contains a full confession. The gold isn't important to me, but my reputation is. Boz has been working the case for me all these years, trying to put the pieces together. He's a true friend."

"What about the other brother?"

"We think Patrick is still in the area. Charles told us that Patrick shot him and that he didn't recognize his own brother."

"You shot Edwin from a running horse while lying flat on your back?"

"Yes, and only his two brothers saw it."

"Are you thinking what I'm thinking?" Violet's eyes were frightened.

"But we have no way to prove it unless Charles's letter points to the man." Obie touched Violet's hand. "Don't be afraid. He would have nothing to gain by harming you. He probably believes that the gold is hidden around your house or property. He might hope to gain it by marrying you."

"And he killed his own brother in cold blood?"

"Patrick was always the most vicious of the brothers. He was only a boy at the time of the robbery, yet he shot at least two of the guards."

"Nick seems to enjoy inflicting pain."

"Has he harmed you?" Obie's voice was sharp.

"You saw him. . .pawing me that day. He twisted my arm and left bruises. See?" She pulled up her sleeve to reveal large yellow-gray spots on her forearm. "I do bruise easily;

but these marks have lasted a long time, and they really did hurt. He frightens me. I've asked him many times to leave me alone, but he will not be discouraged. I don't think he's quite normal."

Obie sat back and folded his arms across his chest, brooding. "I want you to stay out of town for the next few days, to avoid Nick Houghton. He probably wouldn't hurt you, but don't take chances."

"He could come here, though, Obie. He has come before, and when I saw him in town a few days ago, he said he would visit again soon. He doesn't wait for an invitation, and he doesn't listen when I ask him not to come."

"Do you want to move back to Amelia's? Would you feel safer there until he's behind bars?"

"No. I only feel truly safe when I'm with you. Nick is deathly afraid of you, Obadiah. He's big and blustery, but at heart he's a coward. That's what makes him dangerous, I think."

Obie suddenly rose and paced across the room. "I was wrong to leave Barabbas with you, and I don't want to be wrong again. If you ever need me, Violet, give three shots and I'll come running."

"I don't know how to shoot a gun."

Obie looked upset, but he only said, "You should learn."

"You could teach me. There is a rifle in the hall closet, though I haven't seen any bullets for it."

Obie followed her to the entryway closet, carrying a candle to light their way. She opened the door and pulled out a rifle. "This must have belonged to Mr. Bolton."

Obie exchanged the candleholder for the gleaming weapon. "Winchester '73—a fine rifle. Wonder why he didn't take it with him." Stretching up as far as he could reach, he felt around on the closet shelf and pulled out a box. "Here are the shells." Violet watched in fascination and some horror as he levered ammunition into the rifle. "Keep it loaded and handy at all times."

"But what about Samuel? I don't want him playing with a loaded gun!"

He gave her an impatient look. "Of course not. I'll teach all of you to shoot. A boy needs to learn respect for guns early on. We'll store it on an empty chamber." He lifted the rifle to his shoulder and peered down its length.

"If you say so." Her voice sounded small.

He looked down at her and recognized the fright in her eyes. "Don't be afraid of me, Violet."

"You look so. . .so natural with that gun, so tough and sure. It makes me afraid that I don't know the real you, the Obadiah Watson that was a legend in the West."

"Legend in the West? Whatever gave you that idea? I was just a two-bit gunman until the Lord taught me better. I'm a good shot, but I've seen better. I don't carry a gun now, except for hunting. It isn't necessary in Longtree, thank the Lord. You know the real me, Violet. The old Buck Watson is gone forever, washed away in the blood of the Lamb." He stood the rifle back in the closet and closed the door. "Any more questions?"

"Why do people call you Buck?"

"My second name is Buckley, my mother's maiden name. When I was a kid, I thought Buck sounded tough, like I wanted to be. After I met the Lord, I didn't want to sound tough anymore. Obadiah means 'servant of the Lord,' and that's what I want to be. Some people can't break an old habit, and they still call me Buck. I don't mind it, but Obadiah better defines who I am now."

"I like your name, Obadiah Buckley Watson."

He said nothing. What was that look in her eyes?

"Are you afraid of me, Obie?" She sounded confused. "You seem nervous. I thought you. . .well, had an interest in me. I mean, this afternoon you said you wouldn't run if I chased you, but right now you look poised for flight."

Those curls dangling around her face reflected the candle's glow. Black taffeta caught the light and emphasized her every curve. Her skin looked flawless. Her eyes were dilated, mysterious, and inviting, and he could hear her soft breathing.

"Why?" he suddenly cried. "Why would you chase me?

One day you'll take a good look at me in broad daylight and send me packin' with a flea in my ear. I'm no fit match for you, Violet Fairfield."

"Nonsense!" Those lovely eyes flared into anger. "What do you think I am—a proud socialite who thinks everyone beneath her notice? I'm an ordinary woman with many flaws. I'm not looking for a perfectly handsome man; I need a friend and companion—someone to love who loves and needs me. You never saw Jeremiah, the real Jeremiah; but he was no Adonis, let me tell you. He was tall and skinny as a rail, with an Adam's apple that caught your eye first thing. But he had a sweet smile and a heart of gold, and I loved him. That's all that matters! Maybe I was mistaken about you. I guess an old bachelor wouldn't know what marriage is all about. Good night, Mr. Watson."

She swept past him, opened the front door, and waited for him to take the hint. Troubled, he sneaked a glance at her face in passing. Tears sparkled upon her white cheeks, but she coldly refused to meet his gaze.

"Please be patient, Violet. This is all new to me. Uh, thanks for supper."

eleven

"And let us not be weary in well doing: for in due season we shall reap, if we faint not." Galatians 6:9

True to her promise, Caroline Schoengard spread the word about the arrival of Violet's household goods at the train station. Only hours after her possessions were unloaded on the platform, farm wagons began to roll down the Fairfield driveway, each one loaded with furniture or crates. "Delivery Day," Caroline called the impromptu celebration; and people from miles around joined in the fun, leaving their daily house- and farmwork behind to help out a needy widow.

Violet met some neighbors and became better acquainted with others. She flitted about, giving instructions and asking advice. It felt strange to her, having so many people around her house, but Caroline made introductions, trying to put Violet at ease. The Schoengards spent most of the day unloading and unpacking in Violet's kitchen, while Obie and Al set up bedsteads and carried in the mahogany sideboard, several chests of drawers, a highboy, and the davenport. The ladies set up a cold luncheon on tables in the yard, and several men whitewashed the house's exterior.

The children had a wonderful time running in and out of doors without worrying about tracking in dirt; Violet was too distracted to notice them. Samuel played with the Schoengard and Blackthorn boys. While keeping watch over the tiny tots, Beulah and Eunice chatted with some girls they knew from school and church.

❧

Al took frequent breaks to talk with Beulah, and during a stroll to the pond after lunch, he brought up a subject that concerned him. "Is your mother angry with my cousin? He's

125

been quiet ever since he dined with you all last Saturday. He won't tell me what happened, but something's wrong. He's been sending me with your milk and eggs—not that I mind, you know, but I can't help wondering."

"I noticed that he hasn't been coming around. Mama seems sad, too. I think she misses him, but she hasn't told me if they argued. Maybe they'll work out their differences today."

"Not if they continue like they've been, avoiding each other."

"Sort of childish, don't you think?"

Al chuckled. "I bet they'll marry within the month. What do you say?"

Beulah shyly dropped her eyes. "You're probably right. Mama adores him, I know. She's been fretting today because Nick Houghton is here. He frightens her. Did you hear how he grabbed her once and threatened to spank her? Can you imagine anyone trying to spank Mama? He's not a good man."

"My cousin won't let him touch her again."

Beulah looked skeptical. "Don't mistake me, I admire your cousin greatly, but could he stop a large man like Mr. Houghton from harming Mama?"

Al leaned against a tree, tipped back his hat, and folded his long arms. "I wouldn't worry on that score. Miss Beulah, has anyone ever told you how beautiful your eyes are?"

ᴥ

Evening shadows were long when the Schoengard wagon rattled away. Scott, Bernie, and Ernie waved to Samuel until trees hid them from his sight. "Now you hurry and get into bed," Violet ordered her exhausted boy. "Just think—a real bed again! It's all set up in your room. Hop to it."

Violet admired the gleaming white clapboards of her house's exterior. Only the trim still needed touching up, and she had a feeling it would be taken care of without a word from her. What a wonderful community this was! Her heart overflowed with thankfulness for the Lord's provision.

It was pleasant to enter the sitting room and see her old Turkish rug on the floor in front of her mother's cherished horsehair davenport. A painted screen covered the cold hearth. A few pieces of china glistened from the china dresser; much of it was not yet unpacked. Violet stood in the doorway and admired, sighing with satisfaction. It felt like home.

"It's beautiful, Mama," Beulah said over her mother's shoulder.

Violet reached up and hugged her daughter's head against her own. "Isn't it? God has been very good to us."

"I remember seeing some of this furniture when we visited Grandma and Grandpa Carrington that time when I was about six. Eunice and Samuel don't remember any of it. We lived with Father's parents for so long, and before that I only remember moving around a lot. I hope we stay here always. I really like it here."

"I'm glad."

"Do you plan to marry again, Mama?"

Startled, Violet turned to study Beulah's face. "Why do you ask?"

"You've been so droopy all week since Obie hasn't come around. It's obvious that you admire him, Mama. I wasn't born yesterday."

Violet couldn't help smiling. "How well I know! And what do you think about the notion of a stepfather?"

"If it were Obie, I wouldn't mind. I think Father would have liked him. He's kind of rough and rugged, but he's got a kind heart."

"It doesn't hurt that he has a handsome young cousin, does it?"

"Mama!" Beulah peeked up through her lashes, smiling guiltily.

Violet chuckled. "Get to bed, girl, and tell your sister to hit the hay. We've all had a big day." Violet gave Beulah a gentle smack on the backside as the girl turned to go.

"Mama?" Samuel called from upstairs. "Can Uncle Obie stay to hear my prayers?"

Violet had not realized that Obadiah was still in the house. She hadn't seen his wagon in the yard; it must be back near the barn. Trying to keep her voice calm, she replied, "Yes, dear. I'll be up to tuck you in later."

After considering her feelings and weighing her options for several lonely days, Violet had reached a few important conclusions. Although in general she disliked violence and violent men, she understood that Obie's upbringing and circumstances had formed him into the sort of man who felt comfortable around guns and uncomfortable around women. If she loved him, she would have to accept him the way he was. He could never change his past. And she did love him, oh yes, indeed.

He had asked her to be patient—a difficult proposition for Violet. She wanted to settle their relationship now, if not sooner. If his hesitation was due to concern that she could not truly care for him, she could easily put an end to that misconception. She was mortified by the idea of throwing herself at him, but if it was the only way. . .

On the other hand, what if she ended up frightening him away forever?

Still dithering, she entered the kitchen to brew coffee. Nick Houghton stood at the counter, pouring a cup, which he extended to her with a winning smile. "Already brewed. I thought you might be ready for a cup about now. Quite a day, eh?"

Violet struggled to keep dismay from her face. "Mr. Houghton, I didn't know you were still here. Thank you for your help today." She had never actually seen him helping, though he had supervised while the other men worked.

"Have a seat, doll. You need pampering after a day like this. You like your coffee with cream only, right?"

❧

Obie helped Samuel tuck freshly ironed cotton sheets around his bed and arrange the blankets. "I like this so much better than my room at Grandfather Fairfield's house. It never felt like my room, really. Uncle Obie, do you have sisters? Mine are all right, I guess, but they think I should obey them just like I obey Mama. It's no fun having three mothers and no father."

"I have no sisters or brothers, but lots of cousins."

"Where are they?" Samuel climbed up and lay on top of the blankets, for the night was warm.

"In California or in New Mexico Territory, except for Al. He's like a little brother, I suppose." Seated on the wooden floor with forearms across his upraised knees, Obie glanced around the small room.

"What happened to your parents?"

"My mother died when I was five. Then I lived with my pa for a while and we traveled around. I was their only child."

"Was your father sad when your mother died?"

"Very sad."

"I don't remember Father much. He left us when I was little. Would you leave your family if you didn't have to, Uncle Obie?"

Obie considered his answer carefully. "I would never want to leave my family, but perhaps your father felt compelled to leave you behind until he had a home for you. A man feels responsible for the safety of his family."

"Have you ever been married?"

Obie shook his head.

"My mother likes you."

Obie shifted position. "She's a fine woman."

"If you married her, you could live here with us, and we could go fishing every day."

"You'd like that, would you?"

"I'd like that a lot. Do you think she's pretty? I do."

"Very pretty." Obie began to rise.

"What's the matter, Uncle Obie?"

"Uh. . .nothing. I was just thinking about. . .something. You'd better say your prayers if you want me to hear 'em."

"Yessir." With a bounce, Samuel scrambled into a kneeling position, folded his hands, and closed his eyes. "Lord, thank You for sending Uncle Obie to us. Please make him marry Ma so we'll have a proper family. Amen. Oh, and please help me to catch lots of fish tomorrow, and I sure would like a dog. Amen."

Obie picked up the candle. "I'd best be getting on home."

"Don't leave before Mr. Houghton does!"

Obie stopped short. "Houghton is still here?"

"I saw him climbing the attic stairs while you were digging through boxes for my tin soldiers. He came down a while ago. What's he looking for, Uncle Obie? He snoops around when he thinks no one's looking. I don't want him here without you. He scares Mama."

"Unless she tells me to leave, I'll stick around." He ran one hand back over his short hair.

"Obie, was my father murdered?"

"No, but don't you say a word about it to *anyone*."

"I won't. I'm glad he's in heaven. Beulah says he used to talk about heaven a lot, like he was wanting to go there."

"I'm glad to hear it. Now you'd better get to sleep, Sam, or you won't be much help to your mama in the morning. It's late."

"What time is it?"

Obie pulled out his railroad watch. "Nearly ten o'clock." He shook his head. "I must be crazy, stayin' so late."

He stepped through the open door and spotted a startled face in the dark doorway across the hall. Eunice, clad in a billowing dressing gown, stood obviously listening in on their conversation. Caught red-handed, she smiled sheepishly. "I like hearing you talk," she defended herself. Long braids dangled on either side of her round face. "I won't tell anyone what I heard; don't worry. I heard Mr. Houghton talking to Mama down in the kitchen, and I know she doesn't want him around. I'm glad you're still here."

Obie gently tugged at one brown braid. "Me, too. Now you get to bed, young lady."

He stepped lightly on the stairs, shielding the candle with one hand. The house seemed very still. He silently pushed open the kitchen door. Violet had fallen asleep at the handsome oak table with her head on her arms. Nick sat across from her with his back to Obie, head tipped, draining a silver bottle. Obie let the door shut with a snap.

Nick shoved the flask inside his vest and quickly picked up

his cup of coffee. "Thought you'd never come down. Are the younguns asleep?"

"Nearly. Looks like your excitin' company was too much for Mrs. Fairfield."

It was supposed to be a joke, but Nick's eyes narrowed. "Watch your tongue, Watson, and keep your nose out of my business."

Obie's brows lifted. He poured himself a cup of coffee, then pulled out a chair and straddled it. "Didn't know I had meddled in your business, Houghton." He kept his voice low to avoid disturbing Violet. From this angle he could see her parted lips and closed eyes.

"Your intervention here is unwelcome. Understand?" Nick growled thickly. His nose glowed cherry-red, and his eyes were somewhat glazed. Obie watched him with a wary eye.

"Tell me what you mean by 'intervention.' "

Nick swore with feeling. "You've been buzzin' around Violet like a fly around a horse, workin' more at her place than at your own. What're you hopin' to gain by it?"

"The Lord told us to care for widows—"

"Yeah, yeah, I heard that already. Look, you dried-up, flea-bitten, bowlegged old cowpoke, if by any chance you're thinking marriage, I give you fair warning that I laid first claim on this treasure."

Nick let his gaze rest on Violet's disheveled hair and his voice grew slightly husky. "There's a fire burnin' somewhere inside this prim and proper little lady, and I mean to find it. She stole my heart that first day at the train station with one glance from those baby blue eyes, and I mean to have her if it's the last thing I do. She's been waiting for a man like me to come along and sweep her off her feet."

Obie's glance strayed back to Violet's face. Her eyes were open, and as he watched, she wrinkled her nose and grimaced. He quickly looked across the room, at the floor, anywhere to keep from smiling.

Nick stretched his long arms; then he laced his fingers behind his head. Suddenly amiable, he suggested, "You go on home, Watson. I'll sit with Violet until she wakes up."

On cue, Violet stirred, sat up, and yawned, daintily patting at her open mouth. She started to stretch, glanced at Nick, and quickly put her hands in her lap. He wore a wolfish expression, eyes dilated, red lips apart. "What time is it?" she inquired.

Nick's voice was thickly solicitous. "After ten, my dear. I let you sleep for a while, but Watson came downstairs just now. Sorry he disturbed you. Want another cup of coffee?"

"No, thank you. Obie, did you get any pie?"

"Yes, ma'am. Thanks." Then he realized that she was silently begging him to stay and protect her. Their quarrel was gone and forgotten. "Come to think of it, I could just tuck in another piece about now. Caroline bakes a fine blueberry pie."

Violet chattered as she cut another slice and slipped it on Obie's plate. "I must remember to thank her this Sunday. She's been so good to me. We've become close friends, you know. The children and I visited at the parsonage a few days ago and had a wonderful time. Caroline makes the most beautiful crocheted doilies I've ever seen. She has promised to teach us how to make them."

As she handed Obie the pie and sat down, she hitched her chair closer to his. Nick's glittering eyes moved back and forth between their faces.

Violet chattered on. "Nick, is your horse in the paddock? Will you be able to see to saddle and bridle it? I'll get you a lantern, if you like."

"I'll manage."

Obie dawdled over a small bite of pie. Violet's skirt brushed his knee, and he caught a whiff of flowers. Under the table, she touched his leg with her hand, as if seeking reassurance. The bite of pie dropped from his fork, and he had trouble scooping it up again.

The silence stretched uncomfortably long. "Say, Violet," Obie blurted, "I've found a few horses that might please you."

"Oh? Tell me." She eagerly accepted the new topic.

"Kauffman's dark bay gelding would do. He's got Morgan

blood, and he's gentle as a lamb. And the Eversons have a gray—"

"I've been thinking of buying the bay myself," Nick interrupted.

"I doubt Rob would sell him to you." Immediately, Obie winced. He had not considered his words before speaking.

Nick leaped to his feet, flushed with sudden anger. His bloodshot eyes flared. "Explain that remark, Watson!"

Obie calmly studied the man towering over him. "Don't do anything rash, Nick. Remember where you are—inside a lady's home. I'll fight you tomorrow if that'll make you happy, but sit down for now."

From the corner of one eye, Obie saw Violet's hand flutter up to her throat. She tried to speak normally, but sounded breathless. "Nicholas, I think you'd better start for home. You have a long ride ahead, and it's late."

He turned upon her. "You tryin' to get rid of me? You—" He spouted off a string of invectives so coarse that Violet clapped both hands over her ears and cried out.

Slowly Obie rose to his feet and circled the table. "Get out of this house, Houghton. Don't do anything you'll regret tomorrow when you're sober."

Nick reached inside his jacket and pulled out a small gun. Before he could level it, Obie batted his arm up and away. Violet didn't even have time to scream.

Boom. A left fist to Nick's belly—Nick appeared to fold in half. Thunk. A right to his jaw—the gun clattered to the floor. Ashen-faced, Nick slowly toppled backward and cracked his head against the seat of a chair. His large body went limp.

Obie stood looking down at the still figure, shaking his right hand and flexing its fingers. He glanced up at Violet. "I'm sorry."

Violet stared at Nick, then at Obie, and gulped. "I thought he would kill you!"

Bending over, he picked up the gun. "That's likely what he had in mind." He unloaded the derringer and tucked it under his belt in back.

"I'm so thankful you were here!" To Obie's amazement, she rushed to him and wrapped both arms around him. "Thank you, thank you," she murmured, nuzzling into the side of his neck. Slowly he lifted his hands and set them upon her shoulders, feeling her warmth through the cotton fabric of her dress. She was trembling—or was he trembling? He wasn't sure. He simply stood there, immobilized by the incredible pleasure of her embrace until she moved away. Covering her hot cheeks with both hands, she choked out, "I'm sorry—"

Dazed, he shook his head. "Don't be. It was. . .like heaven." Quickly he bent to examine Nick, touching a darkening bruise on the younger man's jaw and feeling the rising lump on the back of his head. "He should be fine except for a headache. I'll take him and his horse to my place for tonight."

"Won't he hate you tomorrow?"

"No more than he did today. His memories will be hazy, at best. He's sloshed."

Violet shook her head as if she didn't understand why he would say such a thing, so Obie reached into Nick's waistcoat and drew forth the silver flask. "Whiskey. I'd better get the team hitched before he comes around."

"I'll hold a lantern for you. I just can't tell you how glad I am that you were here!" she repeated.

He was aware of her watching eyes while he hitched the sleepy, annoyed mules to his wagon. Her presence gave him pleasure, but his hands felt strangely clumsy. Might she offer another embrace before he drove away? Never could he have imagined how good she would feel in his arms. . . . He led Nick's hired horse to the wagon and tied it to the tailgate.

Without a word he returned to the house, slung Nick over his shoulder, and carried him to the wagon. Violet watched as he climbed up, hauled the limp man farther into the wagon bed, and carefully pillowed Nick's head on a saddle.

"I hope he didn't hit his head too hard when he fell," she remarked. "Nick has always seemed afraid of you; tonight he was too drunk to be cautious. You're amazingly strong and quick. You are good at everything you do, aren't you?"

Turning, Obie regarded Violet for a moment, but said nothing. He jumped down, and they stood face-to-face. The lantern he had hung from the tailgate swayed, casting fleeting beams upon her face.

She released her breath in a little gasp. "Thank you for. . . everything. Is your hand all right? I saw you shaking it and I meant to ask, but then I forgot."

"It's all right," he said gruffly. He walked around her and prepared to climb up to his seat.

"Are you still angry with me?"

He turned to find her right behind him. "I was never angry with you. It was the other way around."

"I'm not angry anymore." Once again she rose to her tiptoes and kissed his cheek. This time her lips lingered upon his skin, warm and delightful. He felt ignited down to his toes. "Goodnight, Obadiah Buckley Watson. You are a wonderful man." Her voice was husky.

He stared at her for an eternal moment, unable to move. Then his mouth seemed to open of its own accord. "Will you marry me?"

He thought the silence would never end. Almost he turned and ran, inwardly dying from the pain of certain rejection—but at least he had asked. He could never kick himself for being too shy to ask.

"Yes."

Shock rendered him speechless.

"I said 'yes,' Obie. Do you really want to marry me?" Her voice held a tremor as though she were afraid.

"More than anything. . .but I can't believe. . .you said 'yes'?" His voice kept cracking.

"I did. Here I was trying to be patient as you requested, and then you astonish me with a proposal! I never know what to expect from you, dear man."

"When. . .when do you want to get married?" His voice cracked again like an adolescent boy's.

"Soon. In a few weeks, perhaps." She was achingly beautiful by lamplight. He wanted to hold her, but the very thought of it made him weak in the knees. And yet. . .soon she would be his, entirely his!

"I'll speak with Dave tomorrow about. . .about a wedding." He wanted to say tonight, but that might be rushing things.

Violet nodded. "Good night, Obie."

"Yes, it is." It was time for him to leave before he embarrassed himself. "This is the best birthday I ever had."

"Birthday?" Violet gasped. "You didn't tell me. . ."

He turned and scrambled nimbly to his seat. His chest felt like bursting with the effort of containing his feelings. "I'm forty-two today."

"Well, happy birthday," she said quietly.

It was no good. He couldn't leave, for the mules were still tethered to the railing. Deliberately he climbed down and jerked the slipknots loose. Then, before he could talk himself out of it, he took Violet into his arms and kissed her. Once. Thoroughly.

Violet watched as he drove away; he could feel her eyes, could sense her presence.

Not until the wagon reached the open road did Obie release his pent-up exuberance. One wild whoop pierced the night.

❧

Violet jumped in fright at the dreadful sound. She had never actually heard Apaches on the warpath, but that cry equaled her most vivid imaginings. She turned on the veranda's top step and stared toward the dark drive where Obie had disappeared.

"Obie?" she wondered aloud. She touched her still-tingling lips with her fingertips and chuckled. "I'm engaged!"

twelve

"For the Lord God is a sun and shield: the Lord will give grace and glory: no good thing will he withhold from them that walk uprightly." Psalm 84:11

As she stepped into the upper hallway, Violet heard Beulah call softly. Entering the girl's bedroom, she asked, "What is it, darling?"

"Where have you been? I heard an awful racket downstairs, and then you went outside for so long, I thought you'd been kidnapped. What happened?"

Violet sat on the edge of her daughter's bed and set her candle on the table. "Mr. Houghton picked a fight with Mr. Watson."

Beulah pushed herself up on her elbows, her dark eyes wide with concern. "Is he all right?"

"He was unconscious when I last saw him." Violet couldn't prevent a smug smile from creeping across her face.

"Where. . .? What. . .? Mama, tell me what happened! How can you smile when Uncle Obie is hurt?"

"Obie is fine, my dear. Mr. Houghton is somewhat the worse for wear, however."

"Really? Obie knocked him out? But he's so much smaller than Mr. Houghton!"

"Obadiah Watson is worth a dozen Nick Houghtons."

"That's what Al said. So what did you do after the fight?"

"We hitched up the mules, loaded Mr. Houghton into the wagon bed, and got engaged."

Beulah sat upright. "You did what?"

"I promised to marry Obie Watson."

"Really?" Another voice chimed in from the doorway. "I knew it! Oh, this is marvelous!"

137

Violet chuckled. "Eunice, I might have known you wouldn't be asleep." She patted the bed, and Eunice hopped up beside her. Big, shining eyes peered from beneath the girl's ruffled nightcap.

Beulah asked, "Are you sure about this, Mama? He's nice, but he's kind of old."

"Old? Did your father seem old to you?" When the girls shook their heads, Violet said, "Do you know how old he was?"

"About your age?" Eunice guessed.

"He was fourteen years older than I."

"Oh. How old is Obie?"

"Forty-two. Only five years older than I am. His gray hair makes him look older, but he is quite young and strong. I find him very attractive."

"Attractive? Mama, *really!*" Beulah exclaimed in shocked disbelief.

"Yes, really. You'll know what I mean when you fall in love. Now you get some sleep, girls. We have lots of work to do around here tomorrow. I want to finish planting the garden. Caroline brought more seeds today and gave me good instructions about what to do with them. We'll be late in the season, but it shouldn't matter all that much. I think gardening will be fun once we learn how it's properly done."

Beulah sighed. "Sometimes I wonder whether we're cut out for farm living. You were bitten by a horse, Eunice spilled carrot seeds all over the garden—"

"Oh no!"

"I didn't mean to, Mama. They just. . .flew out of my hand."

"And you can't even drive," Beulah continued. "Everyone has to bring us things or drive us here and there."

"I can too drive, and so can you. I just couldn't handle that dreadful Barabbas. Obie will find us a pair of nice, quiet horses. And once we're married, he'll do most of the driving and farming, so it won't matter if we're hapless city folks. We'll learn."

"Will we still live in this house or will we move to his farm?"

"We'll work those details out another day. I'll live wherever he wants me to live."

"You really love him, don't you, Mama?" Eunice glowed, though her eyes looked sleepy.

Violet smiled. "I surely do. He's a wonderful man."

"What will we do if Mr. Houghton comes around again before you're married?"

"I don't know. We'll cross that bridge when we come to it. I didn't intend to scare you two out of a good night's sleep. Remember that God is our true guardian and protector. Nothing can harm us while He keeps watch."

"I'm not afraid, just sleepy." Eunice yawned openly. "G'night, Mama. G'night, Beulah. See you in the morning." She hugged and kissed Violet before padding out of the room.

"Mama, you talk about God with more confidence since we moved here. It does look as though it was always in His plan for us to come here, doesn't it? I thought it was all a terrible mistake and that you were going to get your heart broken. Did you know all the time that Father wasn't really alive?" Beulah asked quietly.

"I was almost certain that he wasn't alive; but I had to come here, just in case. You know that I loved your father, don't you?"

"I have never doubted that. You were a good wife to him, and I'm sure you'll be a good wife to Obie. He knows God well, doesn't he?"

"Yes, he does. I think I'm learning to love God more as I learn to love Obie. Have you been reading your Bible, Beulah?"

"I will in the morning, I promise. You're right, Mama; God is very good to us."

"Good night, my dear."

❧

Before climbing into her parents' huge four-poster cherry bed that night, Violet finished transferring her clothing from

Charles Bolton's old chest of drawers into a gleaming cherry highboy. "There, that's done. I'll be glad to get this eyesore out of the house." She slammed the chest's middle drawer with a flourish. It made a strange sound, not a hollow bang, but a muffled rattle.

"What in the world. . . ?" She pulled the drawer open again and tipped it up. Something slid to the back. . .but the drawer was empty. Curious, she thumped the bottom of the drawer and inspected it closely. A false bottom!

Within minutes she was seated on her bed, counting a pile of gleaming gold coins. She had no idea how much they were worth, for they appeared to be of foreign origin. Mexican, perhaps, but real gold for certain.

She could hardly wait to tell Obie.

❧

Violet spent the first half hour of the morning on her knees beside her bed, praising, thanking, and requesting wisdom. Then, revived and encouraged, she hurried downstairs to start the bread and fix breakfast. "Rise and shine," she caroled from the base of the stairs. "I have happy news to share."

Minutes later, Samuel capered around the kitchen, shouting with delight over his mother's engagement. "God answered my prayer! He did! He really did! We'll go fishing every day, and riding, and Uncle Obie has a dog. I want a horse of my own like Jughead."

Violet smiled and cracked an egg into the skillet.

Before that egg had cooked through, there was a knock at the front door. Violet left Beulah to watch the food and hurried to the entryway. She threw open the door. "Good morning!"

"That it is." Obie's broad back faced her. He turned quickly and held out a wriggling bundle. "I brought a pup for Samuel. Hope you still want one." He looked bashful, but she caught an ardent gleam in his eyes.

"Oh yes! He will be thrilled. Samuel," she called, stepping back to let Obie inside. "Come and see what Papa Obie brought for you."

A moment later, the frightened puppy was surrounded by

fawning children. "Oh, he's so sweet!"

"Look at the little white streak on his nose. May I hold him, Uncle Obie?"

"Ask Sam; it's his dog. She's a girl, by the way."

Samuel laid claim to his pup and only grudgingly allowed his sisters to pet her. The black and white baby snuggled against his shirtfront. Violet recognized love at first sight when she saw it. "Why don't you take her outside on the grass and let her have a sniff around?"

"I got to think of a name." Samuel obediently carried his puppy down the steps and headed for a grassy spot.

Beulah turned her attention to Obie. "By the way, congratulations, Uncle Obie. . .or, like Mama said, Papa Obie. Mama told us the good news last night. I'm very happy for you both."

"Me, too." Eunice gave him a quick hug. "I knew she loved you right off. She just had that look."

"She did?"

Violet flushed under his questioning gaze. "Girls, who is watching the eggs?"

Her daughters rushed back to the kitchen.

Obie fiddled with his hat, then shyly reached out to take Violet's hand. "You haven't changed your mind?"

Violet only smiled and towed him into the living room. Once the door was shut, she slipped her arms around his waist. "Never." Resting her cheek upon his chest, she felt content. "I do love you, Obie. Eunice was right."

"It's a good thing, since I already talked with the minister. I'm not about to let you off the hook," he tried to joke, but his voice trembled. "Violet. . ."

"Yes?" she lifted her head, but he gently pulled it back to his chest and hugged her tightly.

"I can hardly believe it—that you love me. Don't ever stop. I. . .I love you so much, it hurts. I've got this awful fear that something will happen, that I'll lose you somehow."

"Obie! Remember what you told me about God? How He's a loving Father and enjoys giving us beautiful gifts? Live what you preach, sir." Violet kissed his chin to take the sting from her words. "What did Reverend Schoengard say when you told him?"

"He wasn't surprised. I think Caroline dropped him a hint about us; or else I wear my heart on my sleeve. Could be both. Can you be ready for a wedding in a few weeks?"

"Yes. I don't want a big production since it is my second wedding. Just a simple service will do nicely. The sooner the better as far as I'm concerned. However, there is the matter of me being in mourning. Do you think it will matter? I wish. . .I wish everyone could know that you're not a murderer. I don't care what they say about me, but I don't want people to whisper about you behind their hands. It makes me angry, Obie."

"Violet, justice will come in God's time. If you don't want to marry me under a cloud, I'll understand. We can wait."

Violet pulled back to look into his worried eyes. "I don't want to wait. I was being silly again, Obie. It doesn't matter what people say, really. I know you're innocent, and that's all that matters."

Obie brushed her cheek with the back of one hand, then touched his lips to the spot. "You're so soft, and you smell so nice. . . ." His moustache tickled.

"Do you have plans for today?" Violet asked. The feelings his caresses produced in her had better be saved for after the wedding, she knew.

Reluctantly he released her, but kept hold of her hand. "I hoped to take you to the Thwaites' with me. I drove my buggy with that idea in mind. Afterward we could take a look at the horses I'm considering. I want your opinion on them. Do you have time for an outing?"

"Yes, indeed! Let me tell the girls—oh, have you eaten yet? Would you like some biscuits and eggs?"

"No, thanks. You go ahead, and I'll spend some time with Sam and the puppy."

"I won't be long." She turned back once more. "What became of Nick Houghton?"

"Left him sleeping in the wagon, and he was gone this mornin' when we got up. He's not badly injured."

"That's not what I was concerned about."

"Don't worry, Violet. Go on now."

She gave him a quick kiss on the cheek, but he caught her wrist and pulled her back for a real kiss. To his great satisfaction, she showed no inclination to avoid his callused hands or to shrink from his embrace. Indeed, he was obliged to push her gently away. "Go on with you. . .and you'd best fix your hair again."

Obie took a deep breath as he stepped outside. A wedding soon, she'd said. Who'd have imagined such a thing? He could hardly wait to tell Boz.

"Thank You, God," he breathed, remembering Violet's admonition. "You are too good to me."

thirteen

"For the love of money is the root of all evil." 1 Timothy 6:10

"Before we go, I have something important to show you." Violet beckoned Obie inside. "I almost forgot about it."

"What is it, Violet? We need to be going."

She laid a finger on her lips and beckoned more forcibly. "Just come, please."

He followed her upstairs and into the bedroom, looking increasingly uncomfortable when she closed the door behind him. "This isn't proper, Violet. I—"

"Look here." Violet pulled out a drawer, showed him the loose bottom, and pried it up to reveal the cache of coins. "I found them last night. There were several in each drawer to distribute the weight."

Obie was amazed. "So he did have the gold, and he didn't spend it all. It's not such a clever hiding place. I wonder why Nick didn't find it."

"The false bottoms were fastened in much more securely than they are now. Charles had packed the coins with lots of fabric to keep them from clinking. If I hadn't slammed the drawer last night, I would never have noticed. I thought this was just an extraordinarily heavy piece of furniture—silly me!"

"We'll take the gold to Boz this morning. I don't want you sleeping in the house with it another night."

"Will you let Nick know that we found it? Otherwise, he could come looking for it again. I'd rather have him know that his search is useless."

He nodded. "We'd better let Boz decide what to do next. Have you got a sack to carry it in?"

The flour sack of gold coins, though far from full, was very heavy; yet Obie hefted it easily. "All that suffering, pain, and

144

death over this sack of metal. Strange, what the love of money will do to people."

"What will Boz do with it?"

"I don't know. That's for the law to decide."

He stashed the sack on the floor of his box buggy. Violet imagined that the buggy rode several inches lower, weighted down by gold. It made her feel uncomfortable. "Should we bring the rifle along?"

"I don't think it's necessary, Violet." Obie lifted her up to the seat. "I haven't carried a gun for years."

"But that man is loose somewhere nearby, mad as a hornet, no doubt; and we already know he's a killer. He might suspect that we found his gold. You know I don't care much for guns, but I think we ought to bring along that rifle, if only for the look of the thing. It might make an outlaw think twice."

"If I had wanted a gun today, I would have brought my own." Obie hopped up to the seat beside her. His face was cloudy, yet he did not start the horse.

"But you didn't know about the gold this morning. Please, dear, if only for my peace of mind? I hate to be a nag, but I just have this awful. . .premonition. I don't want something to happen to destroy our joy any more than you do." Violet was tempted to use her feminine charms to convince him, but she knew better.

Although Obie's jaw tightened, he hopped down and stalked into the house, returning a moment later with Charles Bolton's Winchester. He laid the gun at their feet. "Happy now?"

Violet felt guilty. "Yes, but I hate making you angry."

They traveled in silence for a while. It was an overcast morning, yet oppressively hot. "How far is it to the Thwaites' house from town?"

"About twenty-five minutes in a buggy. Jughead makes it in fifteen."

"This seems like a nice horse. She's a pretty color. What's her name?"

"Bess. She's tricky to harness—ticklish. You wouldn't want her." His voice held little expression.

"Oh." Violet felt like unwanted baggage. "Hattie won't think much of me if I've already made you angry. We're not even married yet."

He cast her a speculative look, and she saw some of the tension leave his face.

"What are you thinking? Will it be worth giving up your freedom to have a nagging woman in your house?"

"I think so. Al does his share of nagging, believe it or not. I. . .well. . .I know how you feel about my past, about violence and killing. . . A man should never carry a gun if he isn't willing and able to use it."

"From what I've heard, you're more than handy with a rifle."

"That's not the problem. If you had seen your face when I told you about. . .about my past. . ."

"You're worried that I'll be frightened of you if you have to use that gun? I'm sure I would be frightened in a gun battle. Who wouldn't be? But I've come to realize that guns themselves are not evil. In this wicked world, if only bad men used guns, they would rule over the rest of us. I trust you to do what is right and necessary for my protection."

Right there on the open road, he let go the reins with one hand, took her by the back of the neck, and kissed her lips. "Thank you."

She correctly interpreted his reaction as vast relief.

⁂

"Got some things to turn in, Sheriff." Obie pulled Nick's derringer from his waistcoat and dropped it on the desk along with a handful of cartridges. "Took that offa Houghton last night."

"He pull it on you?" Boz picked up the gun and fingered the polished barrel.

"Tried to. Might wanta ask the doc what kind of bullet was in Charles's belly. I have a notion it might match this weapon."

"I've got the bullet from the postmortem. Looks like your notion is right." Boz reached into his pocket and displayed a small metal object on his palm. "Buck, you'd best watch your back. Houghton must know his goose is purt' near cooked."

"That's not all." Obie tilted the flour sack over Boz's desk and let a few coins drop out. "Convinced? Bolton didn't spend it all."

Boz rubbed a gold coin between his thumb and finger. "He said so on that envelope, but he didn't tell where he hid it."

"You got the report back on his letter? Why didn't you tell me?"

"Just got it yesterday. That envelope was loaded with information. Charles confessed to the gold shipment robbery, but said he didn't kill any of the guards. Patrick and Edwin shot all four of them. Patrick came up with the plan to blame the crime on you, Buck. The letter also said that Jeremiah Fairfield died in his sleep. Mrs. Fairfield, Charles took a letter from Jeremiah's pocket to get your address so he could forward your husband's personal effects. I don't know what happened to the letter."

"I wonder if his brother has it."

Both men looked at her. "Why?"

"Because he must have sent me that telegram, and how else would he have learned that I exist? He probably thought that my coming and exposing his lie would force Charles to move the gold. Charles kept that letter, and sometime recently his brother got hold of it. Nick Houghton didn't 'just happen' to come to the train station on the day of my arrival. Remember, he said that Jeremiah sent him there to pick up a package? He knew that I was coming that day either because he read my return telegram or because Charles told him so."

Boz looked impressed. "You're right, ma'am. I was just about to tell the most important information on that letter. Nick Houghton is Patrick Bolton."

Obie squeezed Violet's hand, and she moved closer to him, lifting her eyes to his face. "You're cleared, Obadiah. And it happened in God's perfect time, like you said."

Boz studied them for a moment. "It 'pears you been withholdin' information from me."

Obie announced proudly, "You're invited to the wedding, of course. We haven't set the date yet."

"Soon, very soon," Violet asserted.

After clearing his throat noisily, Obie gave Boz a slow grin and lifted two fingers. "Two miracles, Boz. Count 'em."

The sheriff frowned, drumming his fingers on the desktop. "I don't want you broadcastin' the news until we've got Houghton behind bars. Hear me?"

ૐ

Hattie grabbed Violet's wrist, pulled her down beside the bed, and studied her face with watery eyes. "You were married how long to that Fairfield fellow?"

Violet felt uncomfortable. She didn't want to lie. "We were married nineteen years ago this July."

Hattie's eyes narrowed, and Violet's heart sank. Didn't Obie's friend approve of her?

"Why would a godly woman marry a no-account cad like Jerry Fairfield?"

"Jeremiah was a good and godly man, a faithful husband, and a loving father." Violet could not allow Jeremiah's name to be so unfairly maligned.

"Then why did he leave you all behind?"

"He wanted to settle here and build a house before sending for the rest of us. He didn't know what to expect from this area, whether there would be decent lodging or anything."

"Something in this story doesn't ring true. I'm sorry to call you a liar, Miz Fairfield, but there it is." Hattie leaned back on her pillow and regarded Violet narrowly. "Does Obadiah know the truth in all this?"

Violet nodded soberly. "He knows more than I do, Mrs. Thwaite. I can't tell you all I know. I promised not to talk."

She saw understanding dawn in Hattie's weathered face. "You promised Obie?"

Violet nodded again. "And the sheriff."

"Ah! Now I'm beginning to see the light. You're an elegant woman, like he said. Although, you're not so pretty as I imagined. You look durable enough. Can you cook?"

Hattie's comments pricked Violet's pride. "I'm a good cook, and I keep a neat house. I may not be pretty, but I'm well preserved for a woman my age."

"Maybe so. Got your own teeth, anyway. And a good corset hides a multitude of flaws. Are your children well behaved?"

"Most of the time," Violet spoke through clenched teeth, managing to simulate a smile. "They need a father, especially my son. He adores Obie."

Hattie nodded. "Well, come back and see me anytime. I imagine I won't see as much of Obie once he's under your thumb, but that's as it should be, I suppose."

Violet nearly choked.

"Obie, come get your woman. She's tired of me, and it's mutual."

Obie entered the room, giving Violet a quizzical glance. "You all right today, Hattie?"

"I'll survive another month or two, I imagine. This lady of yours makes me look scrawny. I'd like her better if she weren't so shapely. Come 'ere and give me a kiss, boy."

Obie grinned and bent over for his mandatory kiss. "You're jealous, Hattie. Now you know how Cyrus must have felt all these years, watchin' you make eyes at a younger man. Turnabout is fair play."

As they left Hattie's stuffy little room, he whispered into Violet's ear. "Mind if we stay a bit longer? Cyrus needs help in the barn. If I don't take care of it, I'm afraid he'll attempt it himself."

Although she was more than ready to leave, Violet assured him, "You go right ahead. We can look at the horses another day, if necessary."

Cyrus gave Violet a sweet smile when she entered the kitchen. "Have a nice chat with Hattie? She's been looking forward to meeting you, Miz Fairfield. I guess you know we think the world of Obie. We're thankful he's found a woman to make him happy."

Violet smiled into the faded blue eyes. "I'm thankful he found me, too."

"I want to take a look at that pulley, Cyrus. Have a minute?" Obie inquired.

"If you're sure you don't mind, I'd be mighty grateful. Now you just make yourself to home while we're workin', Miz Fairfield. Hattie will sleep most of the morning. Sure you won't be lonely in here?"

"Not at all. Do you mind if I find something to cook up?"

"I'd consider it a favor if you did, ma'am. My cookin' ain't nothin' to brag on."

So, while Obie and Cyrus worked in the barn, Violet busied herself in the kitchen, mixing a batch of ginger cookies. That morning in town, Obie had stocked up on staples for the old couple—flour, sugar, cornmeal, and coffee.

"I sure hope Hattie improves upon acquaintance," Violet muttered, slicing ham for sandwiches, "for I expect I'll be spending considerable time here in the future. These people are almost like my new in-laws." She smiled grimly, recalling how easily Hattie had gotten under her skin. "She's a sharp one, that's for sure. But Obie loves her, so she must have a good side."

She pulled out a batch of cookies and slid in a new pan. The table was set with platters of sandwiches, tiny gherkins, carrot sticks, and warm cookies. Lettuce, cheese, and sliced tomatoes filled another plate, and a bowl of freshly mixed mustard made a sinus-clearing centerpiece. Obie enjoyed spicy food, she had recently discovered.

"Better call the men to dinner while those cookies bake," she told herself.

She found Cyrus and Obie in the barn loft, wrestling with an enormous hook. Both men had stripped off their shirts and were drenched with sweat, for the loft was like an oven. "I could bake a batch of cookies up here, I believe," Violet remarked from the top of the tall ladder. "Luncheon is ready whenever you are."

"Thank you, my dear." Cyrus immediately headed for the ladder.

"Do you happen to have any fresh milk?" Violet asked as he followed her down. "If not, we can drink water." She tried not to look winded when she reached the floor.

"We have fresh buttermilk. I'll fetch some from the springhouse." Cyrus looked exhausted, but his step was still springy. Violet watched him exit the barn, his undervest drooping from bony shoulders.

"I'm glad you called him down from there. I couldn't convince him to leave, and that heat could kill an old man in no time at all," Obie said from behind her. "It wasn't doing me any good, for that matter."

She turned to watch him wipe sweat from his face and neck with his wadded-up shirt. His once-white undervest clung damply to the hard muscles of his chest and arms. "I hope it rains soon and relieves this heat. You look pretty worn-out."

He smiled at her and moved closer; then he remembered his condition and stopped short. "Guess I'm too dirty to hug you."

"Come cool off up at the house. I've fixed a nice meal for everyone."

"You're amazing." He spoke sincerely, reiterating the words with his eyes.

"I love you, too." She reached up to kiss his lips. They tasted salty.

"Again?"

She gave him another, loving the way he closed his eyes to savor the kiss.

"Come on before the flies get our dinner." She took his hand and dragged him outside and toward the house.

"Bossy woman," he teased. Suddenly he stopped short, and she recoiled back into him as he had planned.

"Ooh, you're all wet!" She planted her hands against his chest and pushed away.

Laughing like a boy, he fell back. Violet heard something whiz past, and suddenly Obie dropped flat onto the ground. Immediately, there followed the sharp report of a rifle.

fourteen

"Because he hath set his love upon me, therefore will I deliver him: I will set him on high, because he hath known my name."
Psalm 91:14

With a cry, Violet fell to her knees beside Obie. To her infinite relief, he blinked, lifted a hand to his head, and brought it away damp with blood.

"Oh, thank God, you're alive!"

A shallow red crease passed just above his right ear. He grabbed Violet's arm and jerked her down beside him. There was no cover near. She cowered against him.

"Crawl toward the house," he commanded roughly. "I'll follow. He has to reload, unless he has two Spencers." It was a chance they would have to take.

"Where's our rifle?"

"Inside. Hope Cyrus made it safely to the house."

Violet obediently crawled, getting frequently tangled in her skirts and petticoats. Another bullet spattered gravel two feet in front of her. Obie jumped up, grabbed her around the body, and ran for the house, half-carrying Violet. They fell through the door, and Cyrus slammed it shut. They lay on the floor, panting and wide-eyed.

"Are you all right?" She sat up and reached for his head, but he brushed her off.

"Cyrus, where's my rifle?"

"Right here, boy. I've got me a Spencer, loaded and ready. I had just stepped into the house when I heard that first shot. Thought you were done for at first, I did. Hev you spotted the varmint?"

"No, but I can guess who it is. Violet, go to Hattie and keep away from the windows." Obie checked the rifle and levered a shell into position. All of the boyishness had left his face; to Violet he looked hard as nails and twice as sharp. Blood trickled down his neck, but he ignored it.

Violet crept away to sit beside Hattie's bed. To her surprise, the old lady reached for her hands. Frightened for their men, the two women clung together and whispered prayers.

"Cyrus, keep an eye peeled." Obie selected an old hat from a hook, placed it on a broomstick, and poked it up in front of the sitting room window—an old trick, but it worked. Glass showered around him as a shot shattered the window. The hat flew across the room.

Cyrus had been peeking from the next window. "I saw him, Obie. He's hidin' in the brush. See that old stump? The patch of saplings to the right of it."

"Bad choice. No solid cover." Lifting the rifle to the sill, Obie fired several rounds into the patch. A yelp of pain rewarded him. A figure suddenly leaped up and fled, limping, into the woods. Obie followed him through the sights of the rifle, but he did not fire. He could not shoot a man in the back, not even a bushwhacker.

Cyrus had no such compunction. His Spencer cracked once; the outlaw screamed and reeled into the brush, clutching his left leg.

"That'll slow him down," Cyrus cackled.

"Nice shot."

"Didn't think I had it in me, eh?"

Stepping carefully through crunching glass, Obie left the dining room. "Violet?"

"Obadiah, where's Cyrus?" Hattie sounded frantic.

"Right here, hale and hearty," Obie said, "He nailed that feller. All clear now, ladies."

"Is he dead?" Hattie shouted back.

"Nah, just wounded and runnin' for it," Cyrus answered.

"Are you sure he was alone?" Violet inquired from Hattie's doorway, her eyes dilated and teary.

"Yes. It was Houghton, just like we thought. Boz will round up a manhunt for him, I reckon. He's not going far on that leg," Obie answered, leaning the rifle in the hall corner.

Cyrus pushed past Violet and knelt down to comfort his wife. . .and to do some boasting. "Clear across the yard, he was, in that patch of birch saplings, and I pegged him in the laig. Don't tell me these old eyes hev lost their edge, woman!"

Obie's eyes begged Violet to understand. "The Lord watched over us and delivered us today. When we were outside, all I could think was that Nick might shoot you and that I was helpless to prevent it."

"God used you to protect me," Violet assured him. She wanted to hold him, to assure herself that her man was alive and well, but she felt strangely shy.

"I can shoot a rifle, but I couldn't make Houghton miss his shots. That was entirely up to the Lord."

"Do you think he'll come back?" Violet worried aloud. "What if he waits alongside the road and shoots at us while we drive home? What if he goes to my house and molests the children?"

"I'd be surprised if Nick tried anything else today."

She wrapped her arms around herself and shivered in spite of the heat. "Hold me?"

Obie immediately pulled her against him and gently rubbed her back. "I wasn't sure. . .I'm sweaty and bloody and dirty."

"I don't care. I need you." She slid her arms around his body, melted against him, and sighed. "You're good at comforting, you know. I hope you haven't made a practice of hugging frightened women."

"Never. You're no hardship to hold, Violet."

She smiled up at him, then immediately frowned. "You have little cuts on your face."

"From the window."

"Let me clean you up. I'll sweep the glass up later."

Seated on a kitchen chair, Obie munched on a sandwich while Violet dabbed iodine on his cuts and the bullet crease. She knew it must sting, but he never once flinched. Now that the crisis had passed, he seemed relaxed and cheerful. "Attempted murder is plenty to convict Houghton if we can put him before a jury. This time we've got a corroborating witness in Cyrus. Even if Charles's letter doesn't stand up in court, this attempt on our lives can't be ignored."

"If you say so," Violet said, distracted. She dabbed at a cut over his left eyebrow, thinking how horrible it would have been had that shard hit him in the eye. "I'm afraid this one will leave a scar."

"If you don't mind my ugly mug, another scar won't matter much. I've got my share of them."

She scanned his face. "Where? I don't see any."

"In places you can't see. Edwin Bolton shot my leg before I shot him. I also once got into a fight in prison—the guy had a Bowie knife. He might have killed me if the guard hadn't stopped him." His calm voice belittled the affair. He hauled his undervest off one shoulder to display a jagged white scar high on his hairy chest. "Nearly died of infection anyway, but God had other plans."

Violet slid her arms around his neck from behind. Laying her cheek against his, she whispered, "It frightens me to hear about it. Please be careful, for my sake."

"I will." He reached up to hold her forearms in place.

"Does your head ache?"

"Like thunder. I'm glad you nagged me about the rifle. You were right."

Violet lifted her head to stare in disbelief. "I've got me a man who'll admit when he was wrong? The Lord is truly good!"

"Come here." Obie pulled her onto his knee and rubbed his face against her hair even as he grumbled, "Sarcasm isn't appealing in a woman."

"I wasn't being sarcastic. I think you're wonderful."

"You'd better." Amazing himself with his own boldness, he kissed her temple, her cheek, and her neck below her ear. Violet shivered and closed her eyes.

He lifted his head. "Do you mind?"

"Your moustache tickles—but I love it. I'm glad you're not shy with me anymore. I was afraid I would have to throw myself at you. I'm not used to being so forward." Violet traced a heart on his chest with one finger.

He grabbed her hand and kissed her knuckles. "I'm still plenty shy, but I'm getting used to the idea that you like me. Sure you don't need spectacles?"

"I think you're beautiful, just like you think I am. God made us that way, so why fight it? It's perfect."

When footsteps crossed Hattie's bedroom floor, Violet leaped to her feet and straightened her gown. Sniffing the air, she suddenly rushed to the oven. "Oh no! That last batch of cookies burned to black crisps."

"Thought I smelled something strange," Cyrus remarked as he entered. "Hattie figured that was the way you usually cooked."

Violet's brows lowered; her lips tightened.

Obie laughed and shook his head. "That Hattie!"

Looking at him, Violet relaxed and began to smile. That Hattie, indeed. What a character!

fifteen

"The Lord is known by the judgment which he executeth: the wicked is snared in the work of his own hands." Psalm 9:16

Days later, Violet and the girls were hard at work, sewing their dresses for the upcoming wedding. Violet's gown was simple in design, pale blue to match her eyes, with pearly buttons running down the fitted bodice. Beulah and Eunice had, eventually, agreed on pink taffeta for their dresses.

When the door knocker sounded, Violet hurried to answer and found Obie on the step. "This is a pleasant surprise! I didn't expect to see you today."

Without a word, he handed her the Saturday edition. Violet opened it and read the headline. "Crime Solved by Local Sheriff after Twenty Years." She looked up at Obie.

"Read on."

Violet scanned the article with widening eyes. Although Nick Houghton had not yet been brought into custody, the news of his true identity had been leaked. A pair of curious reporters had unearthed a plethora of interesting information, including details that were new to Violet. Unable to continue reading while Obie stood there watching her, Violet asked, "Did they clear your name in this story? Does it tell about Charles's confession?"

He nodded, smiling calmly. "And you don't need to wear black anymore."

"Obie, I'm so glad! I mean, about your reputation, not about mourning clothes."

Hearing their mother's happy cries, Beulah and Eunice came running. "What happened?"

Violet reopened the newspaper. "Read this article; it will answer all your questions."

157

The girls took the paper and began scanning it with eager eyes. Violet indicated that Obie should follow her to the kitchen. Once through the door, she closed it behind him and snuggled into his arms.

He held her willingly, smiling at her evident need of his embrace. "Only a few more days, my dear."

"I wish we had set the date for today."

"What about these fabulous gowns I've been hearing about in painful detail? Could you have finished them by today?"

"We could have done very well without them. No one in town has seen our old clothing anyway, since we've been in mourning all this time."

"It's nice to have something new for a wedding, though, Violet. It is the beginning of our new life together. I'm glad you'll all have new gowns."

"You're so sweet. I don't deserve you," Violet sighed. "I made Samuel a new suit, too. He outgrew his old one."

"I bought myself a fancy set of duds. We'll all look so fine, we won't know each other."

"I'd know you anywhere," she protested, nuzzling into his neck again. He gently rubbed her back.

"Caroline needed this extra time to prepare for the reception she's planning. I know we didn't need a reception, but it gives her pleasure to do this for us. We can be patient for a few more days." Taking her by the shoulders, he resolutely stepped back. "Violet, I brought something else for you to see."

"Something besides the newspaper?"

He nodded. "Come outside."

Violet obediently followed him to the veranda. Two new horses stood patiently at the hitching rail with Jughead, a dark bay gelding and a plump gray mare.

"Look them over, Vi. They're for you."

She walked around them slowly, wondering what she was supposed to be looking for. "They both look fine, Obie. But once we're married, won't I be able to drive your horses? Why do I need these two?"

"You need your own pair. Try talking to them."

Violet spoke gently to the mare and reached for her face. The horse sighed, shifted her weight, and closed her eye. "She certainly seems calm enough. What's her name?"

"Dolly. She's been used as a brood mare for many years, but she's broken to drive. We should be able to work some of this weight off her in time. I don't think a dynamite blast could startle her."

"Isn't she rather old?"

"Only about twelve or thirteen. Lots of good years left in her. I got her cheap."

"You already bought her?"

"Both of them. Figured I could sell them again if I need to. Barabbas brought a tidy sum—enough for her and some left over. The gelding is broken to drive or to ride. He was a buy. I've had my eye on him for some time. He would make Samuel a good first horse."

"Do you think Samuel's old enough for a full-sized horse?" Violet felt a twinge of worry.

"Plenty old enough. This fellow is gentle as a lamb. He's around eight years old, has Morgan blood, and can cut cattle right alongside Jughead. . .not that we do much of that around here. He's smart as they come."

"Well, you know best. I like both of them better than Barabbas; that's for certain. Is there a place for them in our barn?"

"I put Myles to work in there this morning. We're doing some renovating. If we're to live here, I need space for my stock as well as for these two."

"Do you mind living in this house, Obie? I know you aren't wild about it."

"I've lived in worse places. I'm wild about you and the children; that's what matters." His contented smile reassured Violet.

"And Myles is. . . ?"

"Our hired man. You met him, Violet. Don't you remember?"

"So I did. Now that you mention it, I have been hearing some hammering and sawing noises. We were so busy, I didn't take enough notice to bother investigating." Violet felt somewhat dazed.

He gave her an odd look. "You need to get out of that house for a while. Have you been sleeping?"

"Not very well. Wedding jitters, I suppose. When I should be asleep, I keep thinking about all the things I need to do. Also, it bothers me to know that Nick is still wandering around out there somewhere."

He shook his head. "I can't believe they haven't found him yet. Where could a wounded man go? He left no trail that Boz could find. . .but then, Boz never was known as a tracker."

Taking the two lead ropes, he said, "C'mon. Let's hitch up and try these two out."

"But we only have one harness," Violet protested weakly.

"I put Dolly's harness in the barn. No more excuses. You can do this."

Obie insisted that Violet do the harnessing. The horses stood patiently, and she was soon convinced that they were ideal for her. Samuel came and joined them, thrilled with the prospect of two new horses along with a new puppy. He suggested the name "Rollie" for the gelding, "So they can be Dolly and Rollie."

"I like it," Violet agreed.

"May I ride with you?" the boy begged Obie. His puppy rollicked around his feet, tugging at his cuffs and bootlaces.

"If you're quiet and don't distract your mother."

"Go tell the girls where we're going," Violet requested.

Violet's knuckles were white as she clutched the reins and buggy whip, but she kept her voice calm. The two horses followed her directions willingly. Soon they were trotting up the drive.

Recent rains had cooled the air and freshened the trees and shrubs. The road was wet, but not too mucky for good driving.

"May we go to your farm and see the calves and piglets?" Samuel begged. The puppy lifted her head into the breeze, standing beside Samuel on the rear seat. He kept a careful grip on her collar.

"Why not? They've grown since you were there last."

Treat gave them a hearty welcome, barking around the strange horses' feet. Rollie lowered his head slightly and snorted, but he didn't shy or try to bolt. Dolly ignored the ruckus entirely.

"Treat, I'm gonna shut you in the tack room if you don't knock off the noise," Obie growled. At that threat she closed her mouth, but still whimpered and capered around the surrey until it stopped near the barn.

"Good driving." Obie hopped down and lifted his lady to the ground, taking the opportunity to hold her close for a moment.

"That was fun." Violet reached down to pet Treat's shaggy ruff. "Will Treat want to move to our house with you?" The dog's tail swept the air.

"I think she'll be fine here with Al. She's as much his dog as mine anyhow. We've got Samuel's dog now, if he ever gives her a name."

Violet was amazed at how quickly the calves had grown, especially the bull calf. "What did you name him?" she asked.

"Moo-Moo, of course." Al grinned, replacing his gloves after shaking Violet's hand.

"You can't be serious," she whispered, glancing toward Samuel, who was with Obie, admiring the piglets.

"Oh, but I am."

"What about when he grows into a huge bull? Moo-Moo?"

"Maybe then we'll call him Big Mo. Anyway, Samuel chose his name for us. We couldn't call him anything else." His voice rose. "You must like it better than Violet."

"I beg your pardon?"

Obie moved in on the conversation. "We'd better get home now. Al has work to do." He gave the boy a hard stare.

Al only grinned. "Buck tried to change her name after you came, but we still call her Violet."

"Who?"

"The heifer calf that was born the day before you arrived in town. Buck named her Violet because she was so pretty. Once you arrived, he thought you might not like sharing your name with a cow, so he tried to make Myles and me change her name to Tulip. Neither of us liked that name. She's too pretty for a Tulip."

Violet gave Obie an inquiring look and laughed to see him flush scarlet. "Why didn't you tell me?"

"Didn't want you to think I'd named a cow after you," he muttered. "I always liked the name Violet. It's my favorite flower."

"Maybe I would have felt honored," she teased. "After all, she is a pretty calf."

When they returned home, Violet unharnessed the horses, brushed them down, and turned them out to pasture, where they both proceeded to roll in the grass. "What was the use of brushing them? The silly things." She felt rather fond of the two animals, and she felt proud of her accomplishment. "I must say, I do need a bath now. I smell horse wherever I go, and I've a sneaking suspicion that I'm smelling myself."

"My favorite perfume," Obie remarked, and she smacked his shoulder.

☙

Violet saw a striking difference in Obie's reception at church the next day. People who had once avoided him now sought him out to offer their apologies and shake his hand. Friends who had believed in him despite his reputation thumped him on the shoulder and declared their relief at his vindication. Everyone expressed hope that Nick Houghton would soon be safely apprehended.

The wedding announcement created yet another stir. People whom Violet had never previously met now greeted her by name and offered their best wishes for her happiness. Sorrow was expressed for her husband's death, but Violet suspected that some people got a thrill from the solved murder mystery, mistaken identities, and false conviction. Events that had caused tragedy for so many now provided welcome entertainment for the citizens of Longtree.

"It was shocking, the way they had to shuffle bodies in our

sacred graveyard, that's all I can say. We all thought you were a shocking penny-pincher when you didn't buy a marble gravestone for your first husband, my dear, but of course we all understand now. That new marble stone should make your first man proud, if he can see it. I'm sure you must be glad to have him laid decently to rest."

"Yes, Mrs. Blackthorn, I am pleased that everyone knows the truth about Jeremiah. He was a wonderful man, and—"

"I'm right sorry about how people used to talk, Mrs. Fairfield. We thought all this time that you were married to that awful Jerry Fairfield, yet he wasn't Jerry Fairfield at all, but another man entirely. And Obadiah Watson isn't a murderer after all. It's so hard to believe! Well, to God be the glory, is all I can say," Leila Blackthorn babbled at length after the service. "I always said that any man my children liked so much couldn't be all bad, and now I'm proved right. Well, all I can say is, you just can't believe all you hear about people."

Violet tried to smile, but her face felt strained. She was relieved when the woman finally moved on to greet Obie.

"Don't worry yourself about it," Caroline advised, pulling gently on Violet's sleeve. "She'll get tired of talking someday."

"Well, all I can say is, I hope so," Violet whispered. She couldn't help giggling, and Caroline giggled back. They both tried to stop, but laughter kept erupting at odd moments.

❧

"At last, they're finished," Beulah breathed in satisfaction, stepping back to view the completed wedding garments.

"Are you happy with yours?" Violet asked.

"Yes, Mama. You were right—I like this neckline better."

"You look lovely in your dress, honey."

"I love my dress, Mama. It's the nicest ever," Eunice volunteered without being asked.

Violet slipped an arm around each girl's waist and squeezed. "I love you both."

"Tomorrow you'll be Mrs. Watson," Eunice reminded her

for the umpteenth time that day. "Aren't you excited?"

Samuel called from the kitchen. "Mama, come here, please!"

Violet went to the door. "What is it?"

"Come, please? My puppy keeps whining and barking at something outside."

Violet joined him at the open kitchen doorway and stared into the damp darkness. Rain fell in intermittent gusts and wind rustled the cherry trees. At their feet, the puppy twitched her nose and whimpered softly.

"She won't go out, Mama. It's time for her to go out, but she won't budge."

"Try taking her out front."

Samuel did, and the puppy reluctantly followed him to the grass, did her duty, and hurried back into the house.

"I wonder what was bothering her," Samuel mused as he headed upstairs with the pup at his heels.

Violet watched them go, feeling uneasy. A dog's keen senses could detect danger where a human saw nothing unusual. She opened the hall closet and made sure the Winchester was handy. Three shots, Obie had said. She could do that much, though she had never yet managed to hit a target.

Before going to bed that night, Violet placed a bar over each door. She didn't usually lock her doors, but her uneasiness had increased as the evening passed. "One more day, and Obie will be here with me," she told herself, but that knowledge did little to ease her mind for the present.

As usual, Violet checked on each child before going to her bed. Beulah was already asleep; Eunice gave her mother a drowsy hug. Samuel was sprawled out, snoring softly. Violet was surprised to find the pup awake, standing on a chair with her paws on the windowsill. Black ears pricked, the little dog stared into the stormy night.

"Puppy, what do you see?"

The pup glanced at her, turned back to the window, and whimpered. She was too young to know what to do about danger. Her fur ruffled in the damp breeze.

Violet hesitantly approached the open window. Below lay

the kitchen garden, her flower beds, and the back porch, but Violet could not see them through the darkness and rain.

Was that a movement near the porch? She listened intently, but heard nothing except rain beating upon earth, trees, and rooftops. The puppy growled.

Then Violet heard a man's voice. Her blood froze. The voice was impassioned, angry, but there was only one voice. Though she could not understand the words, Violet knew it was Nick Houghton.

She closed her eyes, prayed for courage, and lifted the window another inch. "Nick?" she called. "Nick, is that you?"

"Help me," came the desperate reply. "Please, help me!"

Violet padded downstairs in her bare feet, taking the puppy with her for moral support. Removing the rifle from the closet, she pointed it out an open window, aiming at the sky. Levering a shell into place, she squeezed the trigger. *Crack!* The gun recoiled hard. She fired twice more. The shots resounded through the trees, echoing countless times.

Violet set down the gun and began to cry.

sixteen

"Violet? Are you all right?" Obie's anxious call drifted through the night.

Violet leaped up and rushed back to the window. "Obie, we're all right. Come to the house."

She unbarred the door and flung it open. A moment later she was crushed in a wet hug so hard that her feet left the floor. "Thank God," Obie wept in profound relief. He looked up at the three children, standing quietly behind their mother in their bare feet and nightclothes. "You're all well?"

Eunice shielded her candle from the wind. "We're fine, just scared half to death."

"Mama shot the gun, Pa," Samuel informed him.

"I know." Still clutching Violet tightly to him, Obie reached his other arm to embrace the boy.

"Are you cold, Pa? You're shaking really hard."

"Not so much cold as frightened out of my mind," he confessed, kissing the top of Samuel's head. He squeezed his eyes shut and buried his face in Violet's loose hair.

Al appeared quietly in the doorway, looking tall and dangerous with rifle in hand. "What happened, Miss Violet?"

Obie loosened his embrace enough for her to answer, "It's Nick Houghton. He's out by the back porch calling for help. I think he's delirious. Samuel's puppy warned me of danger. I looked out the window, and I heard a man crying out. He may be dying, Obie."

Obie was evidently reluctant to leave her, but he accepted Violet's offer of a lantern and followed Al back into the rainy night. The Fairfields went to the back door and peeked out.

166

Al and Obie appeared around the corner, talking quietly.

Obie lifted the lantern, revealing a sodden figure sprawled at the base of the steps. Nick was quiet now, deathly quiet. His face was still and cold. Obie felt for a heartbeat. "Let's get him to the doctor."

"Take the surrey," Violet suggested. "Do you need help? Some hot coffee?"

"No, you all stay inside and keep dry. We'll be fine."

Al took time to glance around. Chunks of wood lay along the back of the house as though someone had planned to set it on fire. "Looks like he had evil intentions, but wasn't well enough to follow through."

"Vindictive to his dying breath. C'mon, Al, take his arms. I'll get his legs. To the surrey, quick. We'll hitch up afterwards."

The sick man groaned when they lifted him, but did not regain consciousness.

"Will you come back tonight?" Violet asked plaintively.

"Do you want me to?" Obie paused, water dripping from his hat brim.

"I guess it isn't necessary. . .just be careful, please."

"We will. Nick is dying, Violet. Pray for him."

"I will. Thank you both for coming."

❧

Just before noon the next day, Sheriff Martin stopped by.

"Why, Sheriff Boz, what a pleasant surprise!" Violet invited him inside, but he shook his head. Rain trickled from every crease in his clothing.

"I won't mess up your house, ma'am. I came by to tell you that Nick Houghton died early this morning. He got blood poisoning from his injuries, the doc said. Obie tried to talk with him about God, but he was too sick or too stubborn to listen. Anyway, you all don't have to worry about him bothering' you no more."

"I'm. . .I'm truly sorry to hear that he didn't repent," Violet said softly. "Thank you for coming to tell me."

"We found this in his coat pocket." Boz extended a rumpled, discolored letter. "It's addressed to you back in Maryland. You were right about the letter; he did have it."

Violet's eyes widened when she recognized Jeremiah's precise script. The seal was broken.

"Mebbe this wasn't a good time to bring you a message from your first husband, on the day you're marryin' again, but I thought you ought to have it right away."

"Thank you, Boz. It was kind of you."

"See you at the wedding, ma'am. Obie made me buy myself a fancy suit. Never seen the like." Boz tipped his hat, descended the steps, spat into the flower bed, and mounted his waiting horse.

❧

Violet spoke just above a whisper, "Dear Jeremiah, I still wish you had stayed home, but it's pointless to argue with you about it now. You did what you thought best, and that's all there is to it. I loved you, my dear. Good-bye." She stuffed Jeremiah's letter into a keepsake box and wiped her eyes.

There was a gentle knock at the bedroom door. "Mama, Reverend Schoengard will be here soon. Are you ready to go?"

"I'm ready, Eunice. Just taking a quiet moment."

"I'm sorry. I'll leave you alone," Eunice apologized. "I'm just so excited!"

Violet gazed around the room, trying to picture Obie beside her on the bed. She shook her head and smiled. It was impossible to imagine; yet soon it would come true. "I probably shouldn't have read that letter from Jeremiah on my wedding day. Now I'm feeling pensive. Lord, please help me to be cheerful and thankful for Obie's sake. I adore him, and I don't want even a hint of sorrow to mar our special day."

❧

To everyone's relief, the weather cleared that afternoon. Reverend Schoengard showed up at four o'clock to take the Fairfield family to the parsonage, where they planned to dress. His wagon was soon loaded with people, fancy garments, and the children's overnight satchels. Samuel would stay with the Schoengards that night, and the girls planned to stay overnight with Amelia Sidwell to give their parents a short honeymoon.

At last the hour arrived, and the wedding party drove to the church. Violet gratefully took Reverend Schoengard's arm after he lifted her down from his surrey. Her legs felt too weak to support her. The church building was filled to capacity, and many people stood outside to listen to the ceremony through the windows.

God, are You here? This is kind of scary! Violet prayed inwardly.

"You look wonderful," Caroline, the matron of honor, whispered as she arranged Violet's hat and kissed her cold cheek. "Your eyes are like stars."

It was time. Violet clung to the pastor's strong arm and paced slowly up the aisle, following Beulah, Eunice, Samuel, who carried the rings on a pillow, and Caroline. She remembered to smile. Dimly, she saw Hattie's and Cyrus's faces among the throng and wondered at Hattie's presence. She must have been feeling much better. Voices drifted to her ears, commenting on her gown and her beauty.

Obie awaited her at the front of the church, looking remarkably dashing in his cutaway jacket, white collar, and ascot tie. The stark black and white set off his deep tan and silvery eyes and hair. Boz Martin, the best man, was similarly attired, and manifestly uncomfortable. His jowls had been scraped raw by the points of his collar; his moustache fairly glistened with wax.

The ceremony passed in a blur for Violet until the moment Obie placed the simple gold ring upon her finger, enveloped her hand within his, and repeated the timeless words, "With this ring, I thee wed. . . ." For the first time, she looked up into his shining eyes. He spoke the vow to her alone, pledging his life, love, and possessions. Their audience might not have existed as far as he was concerned. Her hand warmed to his touch, and the heat ran up her arm, spreading through her body and heart.

"Obie," she whispered. The love she shared with this dear

man was another wonderful blessing from God. *Thank You, Lord.*

Guests thronged to the hotel dining room for the wedding reception, where they enjoyed Amelia Sidwell's sandwiches, fresh lemonade, and the cake Caroline had baked. Side by side in the hotel foyer, Violet and Obie shook hands with guests and smiled until their faces ached. Violet wanted to hold his hand or his arm. He was so near, yet so far away, for she was obliged to share him with all these people.

At last the crowd began to thin, and a few good friends stayed to help with the cleanup. Beulah, who had glowed with happiness when Al danced attendance on her throughout the reception, reluctantly changed into work clothes and helped Amelia clear tables.

"Papa?"

Obie turned to see Samuel's serious eyes looking up at him. He wrapped one arm around the boy's shoulders. "Yes, son?"

"Did you hear that I thought of a name for my dog? I want to name her Watchful, since she's such a good watchdog. Eunice says that's a man's name, like in *Pilgrim's Progress,* but I like it."

"I like it, too. I should think Watchful will be proud of her name."

"She warned Mama last night, you know." Samuel leaned into Obie's side, his expression adoring.

"Pretty amazing for such a little pup." He ruffled the boy's hair.

"Have fun with Scott, Ernie, and Bernie, my dear, and don't stay up talking too late," Violet advised, hugging her son.

"Good night, Pa. Good night, Mama."

Samuel joined the Schoengard children. Eunice was taking them back to the parsonage so Caroline and the pastor could work in peace.

Violet waved them out of sight, then collapsed into a handy chair. "Oh, my aching feet!"

Obie leaned toward her and whispered, "I'll give you a good rubdown when we get home."

"Like a horse?" she grinned.

"Same idea. No liniment."

Obie had loosened his tie and removed his coat, but he still looked the distinguished gentleman. Violet ran one finger down the crisply pleated front of his white shirt and watched his eyes widen. "I'll take that offer," she murmured.

"I'll get the buggy," he promised hastily, collecting his coat.

"Ahem."

Violet looked up to find Boz standing over her, his torturous collar hanging askew. "May I. . .kiss the bride?"

"Certainly." Violet lifted her cheek for his kiss. *So he actually does have a mouth under all that hair,* she mused.

He stepped back, flushing. "Never thought Buck could be so lucky, ma'am. You just lost me a bet, you know."

"I did?"

"Well now, maybe not a bet exactly."

Obie interrupted. "Boz, be truthful. It wasn't a bet at all. He made a promise that if God performed two particular miracles for me, he would believe. Are you going to honor your promise?"

Boz fingered his ruined collar. "I already have honored it, Buck. I couldn't sit by and watch such goin's-on without bein' convinced that you've got Someone high up workin' on your side. There was absolutely no chance that this crime would be solved after twenty years—yet everyone in town picked up a newspaper last weekend and saw the true story about the crime plastered all over the front page. Your name is cleared, and there's an apology to you from a government representative, believe it or not. They can't give you back those ten years, but they're sure eatin' crow aplenty."

"That's wonderful, Boz!" Violet gasped. "I mean about you becoming a believer. God has been so good to us—who could deny His grace and mercy?"

"That's not all, Miz Watson. The other miracle was that you agreed to marry this has-been cowpuncher. I don't know what you see in him, but I can't deny that he married you, fair and square. I haven't seen any signs of coercion, so I've gotta admit that God gave him the woman he asked for."

Violet grasped her husband's arm and gave him a look so full of love that Boz glanced away. "Guess I better start puttin' in an order for myself," he muttered.

At last the newlyweds were alone, driving along the road home beneath a sky littered with stars. Obie shifted the reins to one hand and slipped an eager arm around his wife's waist. "Happy?"

"Exceedingly happy, my dear," she sighed, resting her head on his solid shoulder. "It was a lovely wedding, wasn't it?"

"Thought the reception would never end."

"But it's just the beginning of our new life together. Um, is it safe for you to kiss me while you're driving?"

In answer, he proceeded to kiss her neck, ears, cheeks, and lips. Lost in pleasure, Violet responded fervently until a snort from Rollie brought her back to reality. "Aren't we almost to our driveway?" she protested in mild concern and amusement.

"Dolly knows where her manger is." But he reluctantly picked up the forgotten reins as the team entered the shadowy drive.

"I'll help unhitch and feed them," she offered. "But let's skip the grooming just this once, please? I don't want to smell like horse."

"Believe me, you don't," her husband was quick to assure.

A Letter To Our Readers

Dear Reader:

In order that we might better contribute to your reading enjoyment, we would appreciate your taking a few minutes to respond to the following questions. We welcome your comments and read each form and letter we receive. When completed, please return to the following:

Rebecca Germany, Fiction Editor
Heartsong Presents
PO Box 719
Uhrichsville, Ohio 44683

1. Did you enjoy reading *Time for a Miracle?*
   ☐ Very much. I would like to see more books
     by this author!
   ☐ Moderately
     I would have enjoyed it more if _____
     _____
     _____

2. Are you a member of **Heartsong Presents**? Yes ☐ No ☐
   If no, where did you purchase this book?_____
   _____

3. How would you rate, on a scale from 1 (poor) to 5 (superior),
   the cover design?_____

4. On a scale from 1 (poor) to 10 (superior), please rate the
   following elements.

   _____ Heroine   _____ Plot

   _____ Hero   _____ Inspirational theme

   _____ Setting   _____ Secondary characters

5. These characters were special because_____

_____

_____

6. How has this book inspired your life?_____

_____

_____

7. What settings would you like to see covered in future
   Heartsong Presents books?_____

_____

_____

8. What are some inspirational themes you would like to see
   treated in future books?_____

_____

_____

9. Would you be interested in reading other **Heartsong
   Presents** titles?　　　　Yes ❑　　　　　　No ❑

10. Please check your age range:
    　❑ Under 18　　　❑ 18-24　　　　❑ 25-34
    　❑ 35-45　　　　　❑ 46-55　　　　❑ Over 55

11. How many hours per week do you read?_____

Name _____

Occupation _____

Address _____

City _____ State _____ Zip _____

Classic Romance

From the grande dame of Christian romance, Grace Livingston Hill, comes this exciting collection—featuring three stories from Grace Livingston Hill and a bonus novel from Isabella Alden, Grace Livingston Hill's aunt and a beloved writer herself.

Collection #2 includes the complete Grace Livingston Hill books *Lone Point*, *Because of Stephen*, and *The Story of a Whim*.

450 pages, Paperback, 5 ³/₁₆" x 8 "

❤ ❤ ❤ ❤ ❤ ❤ ❤ 💜 ❤ ❤ ❤ ❤ ❤ ❤ ❤

❤ ❤ ❤ ❤ ❤ ❤ ❤ 💜 ❤ ❤ ❤ ❤ ❤ ❤ ❤